KU-311-086

OWEN G. IRONS

SALOON

Complete and Unabridged

LINFORD
Leicester

First published in Great Britain in 2016 by
Robert Hale
an imprint of The Crowood Press
Wiltshire

First Linford Edition
published 2018
by arrangement with
The Crowood Press
Wiltshire

*A catalogue record for this book is available
from the British Library.*

ISBN 978–1–4448–3943–2

Published by
F. A. Thorpe (Publishing)
Anstey, Leicestershire

Set by Words & Graphics Ltd.
Anstey, Leicestershire
Printed and bound in Great Britain by
T. J. International Ltd., Padstow, Cornwall

This book is printed on acid-free paper

SALOON

Diane Kingsley, part-owner of the Cock's Crow Saloon, has made one too many enemies, and finally they've seen to it that she was thrown aboard a westbound train and sent out alone into the desert. Well . . . not quite alone, for, when she arrives, she finds that she has been riding with Walt Cassidy, who has also been run out of Sand Hill, for shooting the man who killed his horse. Walt is desperate — and intrigued by Diane's plan to build a saloon in an empty land . . .

1

'What's that specimen doing here, and who collected it?' Tug Travis demanded. His pointing finger indicated a sorrowful looking man seated on his saddle not twenty yards from the rails of the under-construction Colorado & Eastern Railroad line. Travis was line boss for this section of rail, called Grade Forty-Four on the official schematic. This was the last section Travis's crew would be working on before the line reached its planned terminus, Denver.

So far Travis had kept his mostly Irish crew on schedule and out of trouble. He had done that, Tug was convinced, through constant vigilance and tight supervision. Anyone he did not know or recognize as a part of the railroad was a suspect. Just now the great hulk of Engine Number 8 sat at rest on the gleaming silver rails that had only recently been spiked to the ties, holding them in position. Number 8 had trudged its way across Colorado to this point, drawing its small contingent of cars behind: three sleeping cars for the crew, an equal number for hauling materials, and a smaller enclosed car they used as the cook station. Last came the red caboose where the crew slept. There was room for Tug Travis and his officers to sleep in the caboose as well, separated from the foot soldiers — the track layers: these were a tough, thick-shouldered bunch recruited mostly out of Boston pubs and the city jail, some eager for a steady job away from the crowded Eastern cities, some simply because the silver in their pockets had run dry.

The man with Travis, Garret Sloan, glanced at what appeared to be a stranded cowboy who sat gloomily surveying the vacant land around them.

'Run him off, Sloan,' Tug Travis growled at Garret Sloan who was the second line boss and didn't like being

2

told what to do in that tone. 'Where'd he come from, anyway?'

'We caught him in one of the supply cars. I told him no one rides for free, besides, he hadn't noticed we weren't going anywhere in much of a hurry.'

'What did he say?'

'Nothing. Just pulled himself to his feet and left the car.'

'I still say run him off. He don't look straight to me. He might be looking to steal something.'

'What?' Sloan asked. 'You can see he hasn't got a horse. What's he planning on doing — grabbing a handful of railroad spikes and running out on the desert?'

'Sometimes I don't think you're funny,' Travis said in the same tone of voice.

'Ah, leave the man alone, Tug. He's not even on the railroad right-of-way, and he looks like he's having a tough enough time of it just surviving.'

The conversation broke off just then as the loading ramp was lowered from

3

the last of the railroad cars — the last in line before the caboose, that is — and as the rail layers to a man lowered their tools and stood staring that way, a woman in yellow swept forward to instruct the man inside on the unloading.

What the object inside was, was a fancy little surrey and a big bay horse, glossy and tall which eased its way down the lowered ramp, drawing the buggy after it. Tug Travis took a moment to yell at the gang bosses, 'What's the hold-up here? Get those men back to work!'

Dutifully the men returned to their jobs and the clang and ring of sledge hammers meeting iron spikes again was the dominant sound across the empty desert flats.

'Can't keep those Irishmen focused on the job,' Tug muttered while his own focus was still on the dark-haired little lady in the yellow dress.

'I still don't get it,' Garret Sloan said as the two men walked toward the rear of the train. 'What is she doing on the train, and why is she getting off out here in the middle of nowhere?'

'She was on the train because Captain Pruitt said to put her on it,' Tug said, referring to the railroad's section manager whose word was law. 'As to why anyone would want to get off along this stretch of empty hell, only the woman knows.'

'All I meant was that Denver isn't more than fifty miles away now. If she just wanted to get out of Sand Hill' — which was the name of the last railroad stop they had left — 'why stop now?'

'Number one,' Tug Travis lectured, 'she's a woman, and there's no telling what their little minds will conjure up; number two, it isn't any of our business, Garret. Let's have the train shunted ahead a hundred yards or so. After we deposit the lady at her doorstep.'

Garret Sloan touched the rim of his hat with two fingers, turned on his heel and started forward to inform the engineer guiding Engine Number 8's snail-slow trek westward. Tug Travis stood staring as the buggy and horse reached the bottom of the ramp and the woman, not perturbed at all by what she saw, looked around and across the long, brush-stippled flatlands toward the low, rugged mountains in the distance.

Well, Tug reminded himself — it really was none of their business. He turned away and strode among the long line of workers, yelling at a few of them just to have something to do.

Walking her buggy forward, away from the rails, Diane Kingsley came across a tall, lanky, beat-down man in a torn blue shirt. He was sitting perched on his saddle, which seemed to be all that he owned. The man looked up with hooded eyes, took a sip from the canteen he carried and nodded.

'Mornin',' he said.

'Good morning to you,' Diane returned. She looked more closely at the man. He had a strong jaw and a nose which matched his long face, and just now sported a pair of puffy blackened eyes. 'Shouldn't you be doing something?' she asked, glancing at the railroad tracks where activity was proceeding at a hectic pace. All of the men were anxious to complete Grade Forty-Four and reach Denver where the big city's enticements could be sampled.

'I'm not one of the working men,' the stranger told her. 'I asked did they want me to sign on, but was told they just wanted me gone.' The tall man stretched his arms and offered Diane a smile.

'I've got my saddle and my guns; if I only had a horse to ride, I suppose I could extract myself from the situation.' Diane noticed that the man was studying the lines of her bay horse. She must have looked concerned, for the man returned his eyes to her and smiled again.

'Don't worry, ma'am, I never would

steal a lady's horse. Besides, by the time I could get it out of harness I'd have about fifty men with sledge hammers after me — I don't think that sort of fight would profit me much.'

'Prob'ly not. So what are you going to do then? Just sit there until you shrivel up in the sun?'

'Prob'ly so. No idea has swarmed me. I might just wait and try to climb the train again tonight when it heads back to Sand Hill. That's where it will be going, isn't it?'

'That is my understanding.'

The man was scratching at his whisker-stubbled chin. 'But that would just put me back in the same mess I just got out of.'

'They don't like you there?'

'Mostly not.'

'Me, neither,' Diane told him. She looked around.

'I'd offer you a seat, ma'am, but I don't think you'd be comfortable here.'

'No,' she said. 'Don't bother — I'm waiting for a man. Two men, actually.'

'They're coming to take you away, are they?'

'Actually, no,' she answered with a little toss of her head. 'They're coming to help me settle in.'

'To . . . ' The man lifted his eyes to the far, barren vista. ' . . . settle in? Here!'

'That's right. If all goes according to plan.'

'I have no idea what you have in mind,' the man said, 'but whatever it is, it doesn't have much of a chance of success out here, does it?'

'It had better,' she responded grimly, 'I have gambled a lot on this. How much, you'll never know.' She stood over the stranger now so that her shadow crossed his face. She looked at him as if she were examining a side of beef. Finally she shook her head and said, 'I'll need someone; it might as well be you. You seem to be unemployed, available. How would you like to work for me?'

'To what?'

9

'To work for me; it's obvious that you don't have a lot of prospects just now. How would you like to work for me?'

'Well,' the man considered, 'if you don't mind my saying so, the land around here seems a little . . . dry.'

'We'll take care of that,' she said confidently.

'You can't mean that you're expecting me to dig a well out here?' he asked with astonishment or disgust or both.

'No,' she told him. 'If you haven't noticed there is a little creek across the way.'

'I saw it; it runs about enough water to keep three, four rattlesnakes alive.'

'Of course — but it does indicate ground water . . . I'll explain it all later.'

'I'd be interested in hearing,' he said.

'First of all — are you working for me?'

'I s'pose. Anything but sitting here waiting for some better offer to come along.' He stood finally. 'Ma'am,' he said, 'I sure hope you know what you're doing, and aren't some sort of crazy woman.'

'It's been said before that I am,' Diane admitted. 'What about you? Haven't they ever claimed that you were crazy?'

He nodded slowly. 'Yes, some have; I hope I'm not going to prove it.'

'Does that mean you are going to work for me?'

'I s'pose,' he answered with the grave doubts he felt visible in his eyes. 'What am I supposed to do?'

'A variety of things,' Diane said, turning him to stride along beside her across the barren flats toward the muddy, trickling creek. 'For now I just want you watching my back everywhere I go. As a matter of fact, that's a part of your permanent job.'

'I can handle that,' the man said, his puzzlement growing still deeper.

'You're working for me; I need to know your name — that's all.'

'Walter Cassidy, ma'am. Just Walt to you.'

'Walt will do,' she said. 'I'm Diane Kingsley, by the way; you can call me Miss Kingsley or Diane, whichever makes you more comfortable. Not ma'am, please, Walt.'

'I understand, Miss Kingsley,' he said as they continued to trudge westward, Diane leading her horse and buggy. 'Can I ask you where we're going?'

'You can always ask questions, Walt. I may not answer them all, but feel free. Right now we're on our way to meet one of the men I've been waiting for.'

Walt just shrugged. He was not over his puzzlement when they came upon a man with a horse standing patiently in the shade of one of the scant cottonwood trees fronting the creek.

The lady stepped boldly forward and stuck out her hand to the tall, mustached man who wore a battered black hat tugged low over his eyes. He flashed a wide smile, tugged on her hand and drew Diane to him, briefly engulfing her in a hug which she did little to escape from. Her face was only slightly flushed as she pushed away from him and made her introductions.

'Ben, this is Walt Cassidy who will be working for me. Walt, this is Ben Pruitt. Ben works for the railroad as a site manager. He is going to build a tank-stop station here.'

'There's water here?' Walt wondered, looking again at the slowly-seeping muddy stream in disbelief.

'I told you that, Walt,' Diane said.

Pruitt, who had ignored Walt after their brief introduction, went on talking to her. 'At the most we'll have to go a hundred feet, Diane. I really figure about fifty should do it. We'll have a 500 gallon tank up within the week.'

'My rights to use it are secure?'

'Railroad policy is that anyone who has already settled on the land may use the drilled water. This excludes those wanting it for agricultural purposes, of course. I'll bring back a confirmation letter on the company letterhead to that effect.'

'You going to build a tank town way

out here?' Walt enquired as they walked away from the proposed well site.

Pruitt spared him only a glance. He now had his arm around Diane's waist. It was obvious that it was she he wanted to talk to, not Walt Cassidy, but he provided, 'Just the tank and shelter for a two-man station crew. This is where the locomotives will start to need water. The last stop was Sand Hill — quite a distance away.'

Walt nodded. Things were certainly moving rapidly enough. Meaning Diane had already planned things out very carefully well in advance.

He still could not understand what the woman meant to do way out here on this forlorn land where just now, a stiff wind was picking up light sand and hurling it at them in defiance. Diane and her escort halted, exchanging brief, whispered words. Walt looked deliberately away. The rail crew was half a mile distant, plodding their way toward Denver in the far distances. The Number 8 locomotive sat silently on the new rails, waiting patiently for its return to Sand Hill to drop the crew off for meals, beds and refreshments while it was loaded overnight with fresh tons of supplies which it would return with in the morning.

Line engineers strode along the tracks with prodding sticks, searching for any defects or signs of shoddy work. Beyond them the nine-pound hammers arced through the air, flashing silver before they met the resisting iron spike heads. Other men moved ahead, aligning the rails with heavy bars.

The line continued inexorably, rail by rail. There was purpose to every swing of the hammers, every wooden tie that was positioned. The rail line would reach Denver by men's will alone.

There was a purpose to it. What purpose did Walt Cassidy serve? None at all, none that he could think of.

'Walt?' Diane was saying. 'I think it's about time my horse was watered, don't you? You may be able to find some rough graze out along the creek. I won't be getting my hay delivered until tomorrow.'

Walt nodded. Well, he had a purpose now. He was wrangler for a one-horse outfit carrying a phantom brand. It was enough for now, he supposed. He went to retrieve the horse as Diane and Pruitt walked away in the other direction. Diane was talking with animation, pointing toward the sand dunes which encroached there, toward the far blue mountains. Pruitt nodded occasionally, but moved like a man with a single destination in mind, his eyes fixed on the horizon.

Walt recovered horse and buggy and took his time un-harnessing the bay. He led it downstream a little way where the creek could actually be seen running. Inches deep only, it was struggling across the desert, trying to find its way. Crouching in the scant shade of a stand of dusty willow, Walt got to work, digging out a small crater where the water could pool for the horse to drink from.

Crouched in the heated shade, Walt watched the horse and lifted his eyes to the desert waste, looking at nothing, trying to think of nothing. Poking around, Walt discovered a dry patch of yellow buffalo grass which the horse fed on without relish, it seemed, but only out of sheer hunger. Walt let the horse take its time poking around for younger, tastier grass. He waited patiently for the animal to finish. What hurry was he in, after all?

A man from nowhere proceeding along his uncertain path to nothing.

2

Diane Kingsley, on the other hand, was proceeding at a furious pace. Whether her aims were any more focused than Walt's was difficult for him to discern. If not, she sure seemed to believe that they were. The morning after Ben Pruitt had departed with the others on the train back to Sand Hill, the second man she had been anticipating arrived. He came early while the morning continued to hold its coolness and the eastern sky still held a vague tint of pink.

He was a wide, sunburned man with a clean-shaven face and sharp black eyes, clad in a town suit which might have once fit, but was too small for his bulky shoulders at present. He rode a tall black horse and led a buckskin mare carrying some supplies Walt couldn't identify at a distance. He was accompanied by a skinny kid with a very red face and a wisp of a mustache riding a loose-jointed pinto pony.

Diane went to greet the man on the black horse, a smile on her face. The kid pulled aside a little and sat looking around nervously at the empty land. Diane led the bulky gent back to where Walt waited, watching.

By way of introduction, Diane said, 'Walt, this is Abraham Gentry, one of the railroad surveyors, here to look at the tank-town set-up. Abe, this is my jack-of-all trades and bodyguard, Walt Cassidy.' Abe Gentry wasn't exactly scowling as he shook Walt's hand, but neither could his expression be considered congenial. Perhaps he was wondering just what trades Walt was a jack of.

'Each plot is a quarter of an acre, is that correct?' Diane asked, turning the surveyor the way she wished him to go.

Gentry nodded. 'That's what Captain Pruitt told me, and his word is

God's on this line. Show me what you have in mind.'

Walt was left to wonder and so was the skinny red-headed man who had arrived with Abraham. This one followed after Gentry and Diane, surveying tools across his shoulder, a folded plat beneath one elbow. Walt's eyebrows drew together.

Earlier he had heard Ben Pruitt state definitely that the railroad meant to build the water tank and a shelter for someone to operate the line stop, and nothing else. Certainly no one was planning a railroad town, not out in this desolate country. What, then, did Diane Kingsley and Abe Gentry have to discuss? There was nothing here, would be nothing here ever. The only water was owned by the small desert animals and the Colorado & Eastern. The conditions could support no farm, stock ranch; there was no call for services for the surrounding ranches — there were none.

Walt tried to ask the red-haired man

a question or two, but the kid only shook his head and said, 'Mister, I ain't nothing but Abe's stick man. I know how to stand where he puts me — that's all I know and all I need to know,' maybe indicating that he could see no reason for Walt to know anything more, either.

Maybe the man was right. Walt seated himself again on a low sand dune shelf that he had adopted as his own, sipped from his canteen filled with water from the horse's seep along the struggling creek and sat watching the determined woman in the yellow dress plod along beside the railroad surveyor, waving a hand this way and that. Abe Gentry nodded now and then just to prove he was listening. Then a hundred yards away from the tracks he lifted a hand to his assistant who went trotting toward them, the equipment he carried clattering beneath his arm.

Half an hour on, Gentry was bent forward, sighting though his transit, moving his stick man a foot or two this way or that as he jotted information and numbers on his plat map.

Diane watched for a while, then turned and lifting her yellow skirts, strode back to where Walt waited. Shielding her eyes, she glanced toward the high, bright skies. 'I guess my horse could use a little water again, and some graze if you can find a thing for it to crop.'

'I s'pose you're right,' Walt said, making no other comment. He was after all, only a hired hand.

'Can you throw a tent up, Walt?' He looked at her questioningly.

'Like, what kind?' he asked, thinking of the twenty-man tents the army, and now and then the rail crew, used.

'Just a two-man pup. Abe was good enough to bring one along for me.'

Walt nodded. 'That shouldn't be a problem.' He paused. 'It sure must be nice having as many friends as you do.'

'It's very useful, Walt, friends are the best things to have in the world.' She gave him a small smile and then turned her back to him, watching Abe Gentry at his work on the flats below. There was a sort of throttled energy working its way through her; if Walt looked close enough he could see that working beneath her clothing, and a kind of kittenish pleasure in her eyes as she rubbed her hands together.

Walt took the reins to the bay horse and led it to water.

He was approaching it through the thin screen of the cottonwoods when he spotted, was sure he had spotted, the flicker of sunlight on polished metal. Walt halted in his tracks, gripping the bay horse's reins tightly. His first though was *lawman*, but that made no sense. If the law was looking for someone, they wouldn't have snuck all the way around the camp and to the creek. They would have walked right up to Walt (or Diane?) and flashed a badge and arrested them.

Walt's second thought was that it was an Indian he had seen, yet though one might see an Indian wearing bright metal, it was a seldom thing, such items being rare. They were usually only sported at ceremonial affairs. Necklaces and such were not considered a wise choice of personal wear when stalking an enemy.

Relaxing only slightly, Walt continued along his way toward the water hole into which enough water for the horse should have seeped by now. He tied the horse there, removed his hat and wiped back his hair as he carefully searched the brush around him with his eyes.

He saw no sign of movement. Could it be that his visitor had only come to this spot for water for his own horse? Not likely, he decided; no stranger could have known that the hand-dug basin existed. And Walt definitely saw no horse in the brush; an animal of a size which would have been instantly detected in the thin creekside brush.

Walt squatted on his heels for a minute or two, watching the bay dipping its muzzle into the water, then he rose and stretched and strode easily toward the perimeter of the brush. He darted into it, ducking and bobbing as he ran. There was the possibility of a shot, but none came.

Walt burst into a small clearing surrounded by sumac and willow brush, coming upon his man. The fellow had been crouching; now he rose with surprised fear and threw his arms high in front of his face. Walt had already launched himself at the man before he recognized what seemed to be a sign of surrender, and he felt his shoulder thud into the other man's shoulder and Walt drove him to the ground in a sagged heap. The man beneath him squeaked, 'I didn't mean nothing, mister.'

'Didn't you? What are you doing following me, then?' Walt had his knees across the other's chest and one fist raised high to get in his best punch if the man showed any sign of desiring combat. He did not. The man, as Walt now noticed, was much smaller than Walt's own six feet, carrying a notch above or below 180 pounds. The little man's hands were clenched into fists, but that was out of the shock of surprise and not because of any wish to try fighting back. These fists, Walt noticed, were the size of a woman's.

'It wasn't you I was following,' the little man said in a shaky voice. 'I saw that bay horse and knew it for Diane's — Diane Kingsley.'

'I know who you mean. Why would you be stalking Diane? Certainly not for her horse.'

'I need to find her. I rode up here on the last train from Sand Hill — on the roof of one of the freight cars.' The little man delivered this haltingly. He was still plenty scared.

Walt figured he, himself, looked a little menacing right then with his face all battered.

'That must have been quite a trip,' Walt said, rising. He helped the other up to his feet where he stood dusting off his trousers. 'But *why?* Why did you take on such an adventure just to find Diane?'

'I couldn't tell you,' the man replied, ducking his head enough for Walt to see that his hair was very thin on top.

'I think you're going to have to,' Walt replied. 'My name is Walt Cassidy and I work for Diane — as a full time bodyguard. My job is to watch her back, so we can't have people just popping up unannounced out of the bushes. I have to tell her something; whatever she does after that is none of my business. What's your name, anyway?'

'I thought you'd remember me from the Sand Hill Saloon. I was behind the bar there. I guess we were never rightly introduced. Besides, I haven't got a memorable presence.

'It's Toby, Toby Riggs. I need to see Diane, I really do,' Toby said with a pitifully pleading look in his eyes.

'Can't be done right now. She's having a business conference with the railroad surveyor.'

'Abraham Gentry?'

'I believe that's the name he was introduced as.'

Walt had walked away and now wove his way through the brush back to where the bay horse stood, no longer drinking. It eyed Walt and the newcomer with expectation, but they carried no bundles of hay for the animal.

'Sorry, horse,' Walt said, 'you can browse around a little, that's all I can do for you just now. Don't worry, your owner says she's having hay delivered tomorrow, though I don't see how.'

'If Diane says it, it's true — wait and see,' Toby Riggs, still looking disconsolate, told him.

'Yes. I'm starting to believe that,' Walt said.

After another few minutes as they watched the disappointed horse searching for graze among the mesquites, Walt said, 'Well, there doesn't seem to be any reason to remain here. I'd better take you and the horse back and find out what the lady wants done, if anything.'

'I can't see her now,' Toby protested with panic in his eyes. He clutched at Walt's shirt sleeve. 'Couldn't you just let me have a little time? I'll come in then, I promise you.'

'You came all this way just to see her, and now you're afraid?'

'I can't. Don't you see . . . I love Diane.'

'Well, then it makes less sense than ever,' Walt said. 'I can't see how you mean to press your case hiding out in the bushes.'

Toby looked around as if wishing for a place to sit down, but there was only sand along the creek bed. 'It's no use. All of this was of no use. She doesn't love me, of course.'

Walt knew that without having been told. He only nodded his head as the small man with the hound dog eyes stared at him, through him, toward something only he could see.

'I worked for her for three years,' Toby said. 'At the Cock's Crow Saloon in Sand Hill — you've been there, I know.'

Walt nodded again. Yes, he had been known to waste some time and money in that establishment. He had no memory of ever seeing Diane — or Toby — there.

'Why'd she leave there?' Walt asked as they turned and started back toward where Diane was waiting.

'I don't know. I had the feeling that she was squeezed out; she never discussed that sort of thing with me. I was just the small man behind the bar serving drinks. For three years, I stayed there with her, and she never even told me goodbye. Day after day I stood, waiting, watching for her the few times she came down into the bar and swished by without so much as a smile for me.'

'Doesn't sound like much of a romance to me,' Walt commented. They now were near enough to see the gleam of the long line of rails stretching across the uninhabited land and to hear distantly the hammers of the steel-driving men pushing on toward Denver.

'It wasn't much of a romance, Walt. It was *no* kind of romance. Just me and my dreams.'

'I guess every man has had a love like that somewhere in his life,' Walt said, trying to console Toby. 'They call it obsession, don't they?'

'I don't know what they call it,' Toby snapped, 'and I don't care. I love Diane, and I'm determined to do whatever it takes to make her love me!'

Walt didn't offer an answer as they continued to trudge on. In his experience what Toby had in mind never worked, but he kept his silence. There was no point in heaping more negative comments on the little man's wagon.

Now Toby fell silent; his eyes searched the 'camp' anxiously, but there was fear in them and his gait was reluctant, his face drawn and pale. He reminded Walt of an AWOL trooper returning to face his commander's wrath — or of a tardy schoolboy destined to meet with his principal.

Not a hundred yards away now, Walt had spotted Diane watching Abraham Gentry and his stick man at work, doing something Walt could only guess at. Gentry must have spotted the returning men at the same time, for he waved his hands to the stick man, indicating a work break. Then he began to walk hastily back to where Diane stood beside a pegged two-man pup tent, the hot gusting wind, which had already played havoc with her dark hair, blasted the fabric of her yellow skirt against and around her legs.

Continuing toward her, Walt wiped at his perspiring forehead and asked, 'Where do you want me to stake out the bay?' He bent over to pick up his canteen which was lying there to take a swallow and give Diane and Toby the time to say hello. Neither spoke a word.

Walt said as cheerfully as he could, 'Look what I've brought you!' The woman barely turned their way.

'Yeah, I saw him. Hi, Toady.'

Toby Riggs was a small man; now, if possible, he seemed to shrivel up even more. The hopeful smile on his affable face faded and then vanished completely. It must have seemed even worse than being completely ignored to be seen as so insignificant. Out of habit or as the echo of some long-ago forgotten joke, she referred to the little man as 'Toady' and not by his true name. Toby Riggs appeared crushed and had the right to.

Taking long, authoritative strides, Abe Gentry had reached them. There was a sheen of perspiration across his brow now. Gentry's eyes went to Walt and then to the harmless Toby Riggs.

'What's this, then?' Riggs demanded.

Diane returned a sharp glance which Walt took to indicate that he was not in charge here, any more than a man stepping up to the bar at the Cock's Crow and paying for a drink.

'Thanks for setting up the tent for me,' Diane said, adopting a cheerful tone. 'Did you see it, Walt? It gives the place a feeling of permanence. If we have a sandstorm, or God forgive, snow, we can wait it out comfortably. We can sleep head to feet.'

'I'm a rough-country man, Miss Kingsley. I prefer sleeping out with nothing over my head.' He had said that to appease Gentry whose face had slowly begun to turn purple.

'As you will,' Diane said, flipping a hand negligently. She stepped to Gentry and took his arm. 'Now show me my three plots, if you've finished your surveying.'

Walt decided to trail along. Perhaps it would give him a little more insight into what Diane had in mind with all of this maneuvering. He glanced at Toby, but the short man indicated with a wave of his hand that he just wanted to be left alone.

Gentry guided a chattering Diane Kingsley to the site of her first small plot; the corners were marked with small red rags attached to nails driven into the hard earth. Diane said something, Gentry mumbled a response.

The two then walked to a second plot directly behind the first and a third which was at least a hundred yards to the west. Gentry's stick man, Walt saw, had finished returning their equipment to the wagon and now sat trying to catch some shade beneath its lowered tailgate. It had grown damnably hot.

'We've got to catch up with that train,' Gentry was saying as the couple returned to where Walt waited. 'I'll take care of the legal filing and all that for you. I wish I could tell you when I'll be seeing you again . . . does that blasted man always have to be around!'

His eyes blazed as he studied Walt Cassidy who looked away and held his place.

Diane laughed. 'Of course he does. He's my bodyguard. He has his eye out for anyone who may mean me harm.'

'Surely you don't include me on that list?'

'There is no list,' Diane replied reasonably. 'I told Walt to watch everyone. He's just doing his job.'

Gentry glanced at Walt again, turned toward his wagon as his stick man whistled for him, kissed Diane's offered cheek and then stalked away heavily. Walt caught a few of the words he was muttering as he went; they weren't the words of a happy man.

'Well,' Diane said cheerfully. 'That's that; we're done with him. Now all we have to do is wait for the railroad carpenters to get here. They'll be building the water tank and the station. There will be extra lumber for us. You know that Captain Pruitt won't want me sleeping on the ground.'

Did he? He had no idea who Captain Pruitt was, some sort of railroad official, he supposed. Diane had many friends. He had a thought.

'Miss Kingsley, you aren't expecting me to be of help in any construction activity, I hope? All I can hammer is my thumb — I'm just not cut out for that kind of work.'

She laughed, lightly. 'No, Walt. I've hired you as a bodyguard and that's what you'll remain. I hope you don't think I'm pushy about this, but along with my clothes, I've also sent for a few new shirts and a razor for you. I mean, I can't have you following me around like that. People will think you're a bum trying to put the touch on me.'

What people? He and Diane were the only permanent residents of the place, if you didn't take Toby into account, which Diane seemed not to. The woman was moving too fast, following some inner compulsion. Surveyors, a water well, hay, lumber. Now she was bringing her clothes and some for Walt Cassidy. She was here and here she meant to stay. *Why?*

Well, it was time to ask. If the woman had some plan devised to make living possible on this lonesome endless desert where winter storms could be as harsh as the demon winds of summer,

Walt wanted to know what it was before he risked trying to hop a freight train again. That was the way it would have to be — no man could hope to walk from here to Denver and arrive alive. He still had no horse, and there hadn't been any mention of bringing one in. Which indicated that Walt was to remain on this windswept, nameless, night-numbing plot of desert for as long as Diane meant to keep him.

Yes, it was time to ask. He stopped, stood looking down at Diane, briefly distracted by the flight of a lonesome buzzard across the unstained sky.

'What are you doing here, Diane? You seem to be a woman who always knows what she is doing. But this,' he swung an arm around them, 'makes no sense to me. Maybe I'm feeble-minded, but just what is it you are trying to accomplish?'

'Why, Walt,' she said, briefly touching his forearm. 'I'm sorry. I thought it was so obvious, perhaps because I've been living with the idea for so long. Right where we're standing is the site where I'm going to make my fortune. I'm building a saloon.'

3

Walt could only stand there stunned into silence. Was the woman out of her mind? A saloon, he supposed, would be as sound an investment as someone could come up with. It was probably surer and more profitable than gold claims or ranching. He looked around the flatlands again, noticing their isolation.

Yes, a saloon would be a fine idea. Having customers would make it much better.

There was as yet no saloon. There would never be any customers — not here. He mentioned the matter gently.

'Oh,' the woman replied, 'that will not be a problem. True, we have not yet got the structure built, but as you know, the carpenters will start to arrive in the morning, railroad workers, to construct the water tank and a shack for the men who will maintain it. I mentioned that there would be a little extra lumber, did I not?'

'That much! How can you be sure?'

'Captain Pruitt has promised it to me, so I have no doubt it will be done.'

'You sure must have some kind of hold on this Pruitt.'

'He is my friend, and when a friend makes promises, he keeps them,' Diane said simply, with no doubt in her voice.

Then she moved away toward the little tent, maybe to nap or plan more cunning, unfathomable plans. Walt had watched her closely as they spoke, seeing no sign of guile or doubt in her eyes. She was, he believed, exactly as she seemed to be.

Diane had certainly shown that she was a magnet for men's attentions, though he himself was at a loss to explain why. She was of moderate height, slightly built for the most part, though appealingly larger in her breast. She gave off no special aura. In fact, there were things about her much at odds with classical beauty. Her lips were so full that they appeared to sag when she was not in an especially good mood. Her brown eyes were not even; the left one seemed to drift away even when she was intent on the conversation.

There was no way to explain her appeal if one was not struck by it, but it was demonstrably strong to most men.

Near sundown, Walt as a part of his duty, and Toby who followed after him because he had nothing whatsoever else to do, took the unhappy bay horse to water again. For the bay's sake, Walt hoped that hay did arrive on the morning train; Diane was sure that it would, and he had to be convinced that it was so. She had an extraordinary faith in her destiny and an inordinate trust in the men she judged as friends.

Walt and Toby Riggs sat in the scant shade of a clump of thorny mesquite, watching the horse drink. Walt struggled with his thoughts and then said to Toby, 'She's mad, you know?'

'Of course I do,' the dog-like Toby answered, 'and I find it charming.'

Was there anything about Diane Kingsley that Toby did not find charming?

'If I understand what you mean, Walt, it's that she takes extraordinary risks based on her male friends' promises. But she seldom goes wrong.

'Diane,' Toby went on, 'has assessed a woman's chance out here compared to those of a man, the powerful sort of man, that is, and has correctly concluded that she either had to find the same and fall in with them or maneuver them into where they would grasp at her skirts and be led on into subservience. She cares nothing about any of them.'

'What about you, Toby?' Walt asked.

'Oh, she doesn't care a whit about me, either. But I don't care, even knowing her ways. I rode a freight car's roof just to follow her here when she didn't even tell me that she was leaving. What would you call that? I believe you used the word obsession. I have always believed that it was true love.'

Better you than me, Walt was thinking. Toby was still speaking.

'I talked to her briefly after Abe Gentry left,' he said. His eyes were lighted with a melancholy pleasure. A pup needing attention and getting one brief pat on the head.

'Yes?' Walt was gazing off into the pink-hot distances. 'What did she say to you?'

'She said, 'Well, that's one more matter I won't have to concern myself with. Here's my bartender!''

'That's all?' Walt said, amazed at how small a bone it took to keep some dogs content.

'What else, really, was there to say, Walt?' Toby asked and Walt was at a loss to suggest, except maybe a *thank you*, which apparently was beyond Diane's ability, invisible in her perceptions of the proper way to trample though the world.

'Don't know,' Walt muttered.

'You, Walt,' Toby said after a minute's studied silence, 'You know why I came after Diane. What are you doing here?'

Walt seated himself on the sandy bank. He was silent for a while, watching the lengthening shadows on the sand join and intertwine.

'My troubles began in the same place as yours,' he told Toby.

'In Sand Hill, you mean?'

'In the Cock's Crow,' Walt replied. 'I didn't see you or Diane that night. I let myself get invited into a poker game by a man named Hereford.'

'Vance Hereford — he's crooked.'

'I figured he might be, but then I've hardly ever gambled where one man or the other didn't seem too sly. I noticed that a man with a badge was playing as well, so I figured I was relatively safe.'

'That was the town marshal, Mel Crane,' Toby told him.

'Well, when I sat down I still had my back pay from when the Double B had cut me loose. That's down in the Los Gatos country. They fired me because I kept finding my pay packet short and I kept chirping about it . . . anyway, I had some coins in my pocket and hoped to keep most of it.'

'Hereford had the opposite intention.'

'He did,' Walt said. 'But things went along evenly enough as we had some drinks and the evening rolled past. I saw two of the men conspiring to make sure I didn't get a good card — you know how that works, a man stays in the game just to get the card I would have been dealt, then folds. I let it pass.

'Then about midnight, they must have decided that I'd had enough to drink to be set up properly. It was stud poker we were playing and I had two jacks showing and one in my hand. Hereford started raising like crazy. He must have thought he was being sly, but I could almost read it in his eyes. He knew I had three jacks, having made sure I got them; the hand he was holding was better.

'He nudged the pot with another big

raise which would just about have emptied my pockets. I folded, tossed my cards away and stood up. Hereford just sat there, gawking.

''I don't think I've got enough to back your bet,'' was what I said, and Hereford knew that I was on to the game being crooked.

''You can't . . . '' he began.

''Sure I can. You won, be happy about it.' I shoved all the chips and cash toward him, turned and went out. I heard him mutter, 'I'll get you for this, cowboy.' Then to the marshal, 'He as much as called me a cheat.'

''No law against that,' Marshal Crane answered.

'There was a little more angry conversation at the table. I waited out front for a while just to see if Hereford, on top of being a cheat, was crazy enough to push things further. Then I wandered back to the hotel and went to sleep.'

'So nothing much came of it,' Toby commented.

'Oh, something came of it. The next morning I walked to the stable to retrieve the chestnut horse I had been riding. The animal was down in its stall, one bullet wound behind his ear.

'After testing my cussing vocabulary, I went off, still mad, to find the stable hand. He had just gotten up, still bleary-eyed, his shirt not yet on. He saw me coming, saw the fire in my eyes, and glanced in the direction of the stall. He knew what I was there for.

''It wasn't me, mister!' he said, hoisting his hands. Well, of course it wasn't him — what stableman would be so stupid? But he knew; he knew who had done it. It's pretty much impossible to trigger off a .44 in close confines and not alert anyone in the building.

''There was a man with a grudge last night,' I said. 'You don't have to tell me anything — just nod when I say his name. Vance Hereford.'

'The man nodded then hung his head. 'That was a fine looking animal,' he said. 'Why'd he have to do that?'

''He'll come to regret it,' I said, 'and soon.'

'I didn't think of purchasing another horse. I was in no mood to ride out of town, leaving things as they stood. A man had committed murder, and it was my friend he had killed. Maybe the law in Sand Hill wouldn't see it that way, but I did. In the open country there had been more than one man hanged for what Hereford had done.

'It was murder, and I set out to find him wearing an invisible vigilante badge, toting judge and jury on my hip where my Colt rode.'

'You did find him, I'm guessing,' Toby said.

'Oh, I found him, though it took a few hours. He was standing on the corner with three or four friends, loudly bragging how he had taught some drifting cowboy not to call him a card cheat. I called out to him, 'What did you do, Hereford?'

''I just said it! I . . . ' Then he noticed who had asked and his face went white, his eyes goggled and he slapped at the revolver he was wearing.

'Now a man can acquire many skills in this life, but being good at palming cards doesn't mean you're a gun hand. At least not in Vance Hereford's case.'

'So you decided that it was time to leave Sand Hill?'

'And without delay. I found that the Colorado & Eastern was pulling freight that morning, so I decided to go along with only my saddle left from my entertainment in Sand Hill.'

Toby said, 'Not a bad idea — no posse was going to follow that train once it got up to speed.'

'No — though I doubt Mel Crane ever gave a thought to forming a posse, not over someone like Hereford who had only succumbed to one of the hazards of his trade. He would learn from the stable hand that Hereford had killed some cowboy's horse. I don't think a lot of townspeople would care to follow after me once that information got around.'

'Prob'ly not,' Toby said.

'Prob'ly not. But you never can be sure, can you?'

'No.'

'And look where that's gotten me,' Walt said, again looking at the barren land which was flushed to color with evening's arrival, dry and inhospitable as it always had been, would always remain. 'Toby, this is a derelict piece of the earth.'

Toby got to his feet, dusting off his jeans. He smiled. 'Well,' he said to Walt, 'at least you've got a job. That's something.'

Yes, Walt had to admit. It was something — but what?

'You planning on sleeping out tonight, Walt?'

'Where else is there?' Walt answered, thinking Toby's question odd. Then he considered the source and the spike of fury Abe Gentry had shown when Diane had suggested to Walt that he could share the two-man tent with her. It seemed that Diane Kingsley had as many jealous suitors as she did friends.

'Nowhere, I guess,' Toby said. The last sundown hues of pink and red were dripping from the sky into the gloom black of night. 'Better keep your eyes open,' he puffed as they started up a sand hill.

'I know.'

'I wasn't sure if you had spotted him or not.'

'I did,' Walt Cassidy replied. Open desert was not a good place to try to sneak up on folks, and Walt had twice spotted the man with the rifle who was trying to Indian his way toward their camp that day.

Who? Why? There was no telling — unless Diane could tell him something about the uninvited visitor, but she was a woman who held her own secrets closely.

For one thing, she had not ever said a word about why she had left Sand Hill on the run, and it had to be that she did just that. She was great at organizing on the run, but she seemed to have had little choice about it. She had arrived with nearly nothing; there was most likely trouble on her back trail as well . . .

Men don't go skulking around on the desert at night, toting a Winchester for no reason.

He would have to ask Diane, whether she liked answering or not. It could be important to keeping Diane — and himself — alive. There are only a few causes to wish to commit murder: love, hate or money. With Diane Kingsley, Walt reflected, it could be any or all of these.

When he finally got up the nerve to talk to the woman, he found her seated in front of her tent with a lighted lantern beside her. Where had she gotten that? He squatted in front of her and watched her face through the smoky illumination.

'Boss,' he began, tipping his hat back, 'we should have a talk.'

'I thought we had agreed that you were to address me as Diane or Miss

Kingsley,' she said in a neutral voice. She was looking directly at him, her smile slight. Her wandering eye drifted a little, but she brought it under control.

'We did, Miss Kingsley, I sort of forgot.' His eyes squinted at the lantern light. 'I thought that you should know that there's an armed man out there, trying to approach the camp in the darkness.'

'Well, that's to be expected,' Diane said with seeming indifference. 'After all, that's what I hired you for, isn't it?'

'You can't expect me to go out there and track him?'

'No, of course not,' she said as it were a matter of indifference to her, 'he'll come in one day; you can take care of him then.'

'All right,' Walt answered, giving it up, since he seriously did not want to go out on the desert pursuing a stealthy man. 'You know who he is then?'

'Of course,' she answered. 'But that's

something you don't need to know.'

'Of course not,' Walt said a little grumpily. Realizing why that was so, he did add, 'Diane, I haven't had a bite to eat since I've been here; it makes me a little testy.'

'I know that — ask Toby, he's bound to have carried something away. This will all be a thing of the past tomorrow when my supplies start arriving.'

Would it? Walt could only hope so and take the woman at her word. He got to his feet to walk off and see if maybe the little man did have something in the way of food that he'd be willing to share. It was wacky to be working for a woman who couldn't even supply the necessities for a man's survival, but Walt reflected, she had never promised him anything at all, but a job. Yet it seemed to Walt that with this woman, if she had promised him champagne and T-bone steaks on the next day, he would have believed her.

She was that kind of woman. Diane

4

The train arrived with the early light of dawn — a behemoth appearing out of the glow and glare of the morning sun. There was the usual gang of Irishmen on the work train. Looking fit and eager for a day's work laying rail — though such was probably not the case; they worked for their pay, and they were in between the comforts of a town now. Far from Sand Hill, far distant from Denver. The desert landscape was far different, more forbidding, than any they had known before. Different than the bustling Eastern cities, certainly mysterious and more threatening in appearance than their faraway green island home.

The land was red, long, devoid of water as had been proven to them, with here and there groups of un-pacified Indians and assorted bad men running from one spot of trouble to another.

The train made its labored way into the water stop, squealed to a halt and settled into steely silence as the laborers with a purpose slipped from their berths and methodically began unloading the goods the iron horse carried.

Diane had promised that supplies would be delivered; they were. She stood watching the work with an enigmatic smile.

Before the sun was fully up, the place was alive with railroad workers, carpenters and laborers. A huge, 5,000 gallon water tank, pre-assembled somewhere else, was ready to be carefully offloaded at the chosen site, along with the sections of the windmill. The man who had first selected the location, Ben Pruitt, had returned with a short team of well diggers. One of the other flat-cars carried neatly stacked finished lumber in prodigious amounts. The flat-car behind this one was similarly laden. Not really to Walt Cassidy's surprise, but to his interest was that the lumber was unloaded at two different locations — the first at the water tank site, the second where Diane stood watching her chosen lot. Her expression varied from knowing, to concerned, to pleased.

Ben Pruitt came by just after nine o'clock and announced loudly, 'They've hit water at fifty feet, just like I told you! Pump's ready to go!' He removed his hat to wipe his brow as Diane clung to his neck with girlish glee. They whispered together and Walt saw Pruitt glance around at the ongoing work and say, 'Not now, I don't think.'

Walt didn't wonder at the meaning of that exchange; it was none of his affair. But the short man, Toby who stood at his side now, wearing a red vest and new white shirt — presumably his bartender's outfit — muttered what might have been a small muffled curse — and turned away saying, 'Well, what could I expect? I've nothing to give her.'

The man was paying a heavy price for his one-sided love.

Deciding that Diane was in no immediate need of his bodyguard services, Walt once again took the bay horse and led it upstream to the waterhole he had dug, thinking to himself that this might be the last time such a service would be required. The well had been dug, the pump installed. The water tower was in the last stages of construction. By evening they might actually be able to consider this place a water stop. Walt thought that, oddly, he would miss his simple task. It was pleasant being alone along the ribbon of a creek trickling its way through the chaparral.

He needed a horse!

Walt watched the bay dip its muzzle into the accustomed muddy tank and thought again, I need a horse. Not Diane's buggy-trained town horse, of course. Besides, he could never consider taking it. Such a move would be a betrayal. Where then could he come by one? Could he somehow have a horse brought out from Sand Hill? Of course

— all things being possible. If a man had the money; Walt Cassidy had not a nickel to his name, and it seemed highly unlikely that he would be coming by any soon. He and Diane had never gotten far enough along in their conversations to discuss a small matter like his wages, if any.

'You've dug yourself quite a pit, Walt Cassidy,' he said to himself and to the bay horse which was uninterested.

He let another warm, bright hour drift past before he again rose and started back toward the camp. It was plain shocking to find what it had become.

Walt had known of gold rush camps thrown up in no time. Wandering the mountains, a man can come upon groups of buildings where none had been a month, a week earlier. The railroad, it seemed, had those rough, country citifiers out-classed by miles. The new water tank had been raised, the windmill affixed, and half a dozen carpenters were finishing the bracing of the tower. Beside the tank, set a little back from the rails, another group of men were laying flooring for the shelter of the water-stop crew. Of course, they had built many such as these, and worked now according to a familiar scheme. Still the tank and the shelter were going up at a phenomenal rate. The hammers rang in a staccato chorus, saws chirped and buzzed through the green pine lumber, and the new timber shone as if burnished, as it was smoothed by long, sharp planes in capable hands. Walt stood as if transfixed for a while, amazed at the deft plying of the tools. As he had told Diane, his hands were unused to using saw and hammer without injury to himself. Then again, he thought, he was probably better than any man among them when he shook out a loop.

Walt saw two men in town suits wandering the worksite, shouting helpful words where none were needed. These workmen obviously knew their work well, and could probably manage their jobs in their sleep.

Still, a boss always has to feel that he's contributing something even when he's just getting in the way.

One of the two men, Walt saw, was Ben Pruitt, the well diggers' chief whose part in the affair was presumably at an end. He would be proceeding to the next proposed site to see if it were suitable. The second man was vaguely familiar; Walt only recognized him with certainty when one of the carpenters, a burly Swede, called out to him by name. It was Tug Travis, the number two line boss.

'We can't wait any longer for these men,' Travis said irritably. 'They've got enough material to keep them busy. We'll just have to pick them up on the way back! We've got some steel to spike down before day is done. I told Captain Pruitt that we could make ten easy miles today out on the flats.'

The two men continued on toward the Number Eight locomotive, Tug Travis ranting, waving his hands, Pruitt nodding dutifully.

It seemed to Walt that the frenetic building activity around him slowed just a little. The track layers sitting in the scant shade cast by the freight cars got to their feet, stretching, tugging their hats down against the sun-glare. They had been enjoying watching other men laboring through the heat. Now it was their turn.

Walt stood watching as the train pulled out once more. Near Diane's 'saloon' he noticed men working. Supplies from the train were carried nearer. A couple of carpenters with a chalk line were laying out the floor plan for the building. The railroad men were going to build it for her? The woman had many friends in high places, it seemed.

He supposed it didn't matter much to the carpenters. They were going to be there all day anyway.

'What's that supposed to be?' a voice at Walt's shoulder asked.

'The saloon, of course,' Walt replied.

'No, really?'

'Really,' Walt said turning to face the short round man with a pipe in his mouth, his cherry red face wreathed in smiles. He wore a leather vest over bib overalls and cracked farm boots.

'My name's Clyde Waring,' the man said, thrusting out a chubby, sun-cracked hand.

'Pleased to meet you. You're a part of the rail-road's crew?'

'Me?' Clyde Waring laughed and nodded. 'I'm all of the crew for the water stop. Until they can find me a man to help out. That won't be easy. Not many want to live out on the desert all alone like this. We call those men spiders. They climb up on the tower and lower the spigot for the train's boilers. In between they watch the water level, chop firewood and cook. It's not a bad job, but no spider ever lasts long. It's the sheer boredom that gets them.

'I've had a few Indian helpers — they're the best. Willing to work hard for a few dollars, unused to civilization so they don't know what they might be missing way out here.'

A carpenter, finished with his work, leaped down from the water tank's high platform behind them.

'You didn't say who you were,' Clyde said, 'nor what you're doing way out here. Not looking for work, are you?'

'No, I've got a job — or so I'm told.' He smiled. 'I'd be of no use to the railroad anyway. I work for the lady who owns the saloon.'

Clyde only nodded. 'Nice horse you've got,' he said for something to say. Walt told him, 'It's not mine; it belongs to the lady. I was out watering it.'

'Well, that's a thing of the past, at least.'

'What do you mean?' Walt asked. Clyde inclined his head toward the water tank. 'Come along with me,' he said and together, they strode toward the tank, dodging workmen. Clyde halted and said, 'Do you see that?'

He was pointing at a two-inch galvanized pipe which depended from the water tank. It had a red steel valve attached to it.

'You can get your water out of there from now on, just like we are going to do. We were reminded that anyone in residence before we put our well in was to have equal access to the water — barring agricultural users. That includes your boss, doesn't it? In fact, she's the only one I see that does apply to.

'Have you got buckets?' Clyde asked. 'If not I can let you have a couple of new ones. They always ship out more than I need.'

'I'd appreciate that.'

'Don't give it a thought — what are neighbors for?'

The men around them now were scuttling off toward Diane's location; a few of them looked furtively over their shoulders, which was totally unnecessary — no boss was around for at least a hundred miles to watch them.

'Where do you think they're going?' Clyde asked in puzzlement.

'I'm pretty sure I know,' Walt told the red-faced man, 'knowing my boss.'

Shrugging, Clyde Waring followed Walt and the led horse in the direction indicated by the carpenters and loading crew who streamed that way like ants across the sand.

'Didn't take word long to make its way through the camp, did it?' Walt commented.

Clyde Waring, still baffled, shook his head. 'Though there is a sight I would have walked off the job for.'

Walt glanced in the direction Clyde's eyes indicated to see Diane Kingsley in a white dress with a red ribbon at its waist, her dark hair brushed to a gloss and pinned up in some intricate fashion. How had she managed that? Walt could only wonder at the ways of this woman. She was smiling broadly now, apparently pleased with herself. Beneath the shelf of rock she stood on, three whiskey barrels rested in a row, supporting a wide plank. Behind this makeshift contraption, stood Toby Riggs in his white shirt and red vest, drawing whiskey from a fourth barrel. Business was brisk. Every time a railroad man slapped a dime down on the plank it was whisked away by Toby and replaced by a small glass of whiskey.

'They won't be getting much work done after this,' Clyde muttered, though his only concern could be that his line shack was not going to be completed that day.

'They've done quite a bit already,' Walt said. It was not exactly what they were being paid for, but beyond them a proper building was being raised. Already the uprights supported ceiling beams, and extensions rose to support a second floor. A wooden floor was being laid as well. Occasionally one of the carpenters would detach himself from the work crew and return to Toby's make-do bar to drink another whiskey.

'I'll be a sumbitch,' Clyde Waring

mumbled in what was a strong curse for him. 'I guess we should help christen the place, don't you, Walt?' he asked with a grin.

'I'll wait — go ahead, Clyde. I want to talk to my boss.'

Clyde grinned, briefly placed his hand on Walt's shoulder and made his way down the shallow slope to slap his own coin on the plank. Toby glanced up at the new customer, at Walt Cassidy standing there with Diane's horse but never broke his rhythm as he served one drink after another. Walt plodded through the sand to where Diane Kingsley stood observing the activity below her.

Tilting back his hat, Walt asked, 'Where do you want your horse?'

'You can drop his anchor behind the tent, beside the buggy,' she said with indifference. 'I won't be using it for a while.'

'Want to sell it?' Walt asked.

'Have you got any money?' she asked with a teasing smile.

70

'Not until I get paid,' Walt answered, 'which was another thing I wanted to talk to you about.'

'Another thing?' Diane asked, turning toward him. It was a deft way to side-step the unasked question in Walt's mind. 'What else did you want to talk about, Walt?' Then she gave him a smile he had never seen from the woman, it was warm, questioning and welcoming. Her eyes seemed to grow misty — he guessed that this was her working smile, the one she used for softening men's hearts and making more 'friends'.

'Nothing else right now,' he said, keeping a grip on himself. 'Right now, getting a horse and riding out of here is the main topic on my mind.'

'Of course it is, Walt.' Her expression had grown understanding. He decided that if the woman had ever set her mind to it, she could have become a great actress. Of course, in Walt's mind, all females were actresses.

She took him by the arm and walked with him down to the flats and the new building which was rapidly rising as the drinking carpenters worked on it furiously. They had to speak above the bang of the hammers.

'It looks like you've gotten yourself a start,' Walt told the lady, 'though I can't see how you expect to make a go of it — way out here on the desert flats without even a town around to support you.'

'It will do fine,' Diane told him — either because she firmly believed it or needed to. 'You'll see, Walt.' She stopped and looked up into his eyes. She looked away again and spread her arms. 'They said I couldn't do it, but now what do you see standing before you?'

She paused, her eyes glitter-bright.

'My saloon!'

5

A few weeks on, nothing had changed in Walt's world despite the fact that Diane Kingsley continued to build her tiny empire almost obsessively. That is with the exception of considering him — he still did not have a horse to ride, to escape on. Diane had explained that in multiple ways, none on which carried much weight with Walt.

'But you have a job here with me, Walt. I need you around. If I bought you a horse — assuming I could do that, why, I'd never know when you were about to run out on me!'

'You ought to leave that up to me,' Walt objected.

'Besides,' Diane said, smiling as she continued to clutch his arm, 'where else would you rather be?'

'Than here? Just about anywhere.'

'Like alone out on the desert — that

73

would be foolish, wouldn't it? Look around at how things are sprouting, Walt! You have a roof over your head and a hot meal anytime you like now!'

Well, that was nearly true. The work on the eastern end of the roof had not been completed. The only way to get a hot meal was to ask Toby to cook it over the stove — which was a sheet of rolled iron over adobe blocks. Toby was required to spend most of his waking hours piecing together the interior of the unfinished saloon. Poor Toby had enough problems without Walt asking him to do his cooking for him. For the time being there was a mountain of tinned goods and three whole hams, forty to fifty pound sacks of potatoes and some assorted dried food, all of which looked pretty good when it was first delivered off the train, but started to pale as a regular diet.

The roof was the biggest problem, of course, for the train line did not need workers at the site any longer and so

Number Eight now paused at the station only for a sip of water and then thundered its way on toward Denver.

The Number Eight locomotive returned again just before sunset with its weary line crew, watered, and steamed away. Walt had seen the thirsty men looking longingly toward Diane's saloon, prompting him to ask Clyde Waters, 'How long is the stop in all?'

'We average something less than half an hour, time enough for me to scale that damned ladder — I *still* haven't gotten me a spider, and I'm too old to work this place alone. That's time enough for me to do the job and let those who must step out and go behind a bush for a few minutes.'

'Not time enough for them to get a drink at Diane's, though?'

'No, but there are some who wish for it by the time they reach the end a long day's work.'

'I imagine.'

'Yes, well that thirty minute stop isn't long enough for me to do my job properly — it's like plugging a bottle in a baby's mouth as it's wheeled past. I told Diane that I need more time or a spider, or both!'

'You spoke to Diane!' Walt asked with obvious surprise.

'Sure — she's got a stake in this too. If them laborers had an extra thirty minutes, they'd stampede down to the saloon when the train stopped. It would benefit all parties to have a full hour's stop.'

'I suppose so, but I don't get you, Clyde. Why would you go to Diane with a railroad problem?'

Clyde, in blue overalls, leaned against the wall of the water station, hands in pockets and smiled, 'Well, son, she is the closest thing we've got to a working line boss.'

'What about Tug Travis?' Walt enquired.

'I said a *working* boss,' Clyde said, turning his head to spit.

'But that's hardly what Diane is,' Walt protested.

'Isn't she? I'd say she kind of has

been that since the day she met Captain Pruitt.'

That was something Walt could have thought long about, but he didn't have the inclination. He said, 'I hope you get your spider soon,' and left Clyde to his solitary station.

The saloon was still the only structure but for the water station. It must have been visible for fifty miles considering the flat land around it, but it saw no customers, no curious visitors, for the truth was that there was nothing to be seen unless a man liked peering long into the bottom of a whiskey glass, and there were no other residents of the long land. He wondered again how Diane hoped, no — was certain — that she could make the venture work out here.

The plot for the building on the lot directly behind the saloon had been marked out with pegs and twine.

'This, of course, is the hotel,' she had told Walt as she always did, in her own time and as if he were an exceptionally slow student. 'It will be only one storey high; we shan't need that many rooms.'

'But you're planning on upstairs rooms at the saloon,' he pointed out. She paused, sighed, and looked skyward for help.

'Yes, but we can't have the men who might be getting drunk and rambunctious staying in the saloon, nor can we have those who wish not to be bothered housed beside them. Any man who may find himself in an unhappy position of drunkenness without the ability to maintain decorum will be tossed out the back door of the saloon . . . '

'Finding himself directly in front of the hotel provided,' Walt finished for her. She smiled and walked slowly on.

'Simple, is it not?'

'I suppose, if you say so.' She hadn't said a word about who was to do the tossing out of rambunctious men. 'Which building will you be sleeping in, Diane? Surely not the . . . ?'

'I shall abide upstairs in the saloon

only until my own house is completed.' Well, the saloon wasn't finished itself yet, especially not the upstairs. In her own house?

'Over there, Walt. Don't you remember that I had a third lot staked out when Abraham Gentry was here?'

'Yes, I do,' Walt responded. 'You mean, don't you, the one a hundred yards away?'

Walt had wanted to say 'all the way across town', but there being no town, did not.

'Of course — that's the one. A person has a difficult enough time of it working in a saloon without having to actually live in the place.'

Walt agreed. Actually there was no house being built and as of now the upper story of the saloon stood gaunt, bare, and mostly empty with no sign of any working carpenters, but Diane would have her visions, and most of them seemed to come true.

Walt approached her over the question of time which could force the saloon to wither and die before it was even truly started. If no one could drink, nothing could be sold. As Walt spoke, he again encountered the feeling that he was asking Diane about obvious problems with obvious solutions.

'I'll send a letter back to Captain Pruitt in Sand Hill — I obviously can't return there myself yet . . . '

'Of course not,' Walt muttered, not knowing why. If the woman ever wrote her life story, it would be one sentence at a time.

'I will just tell him that Clyde cannot possibly do all that he is required to do all by himself within half an hour.'

'That should do it,' Walt grumbled as they again reached the back door of the saloon — one which was not yet hung.

'Oh, I know it will,' Diane said brightly, wiping back a vagrant strand of blond hair.

'Then everything will fall into place. The railroad will stop by each evening and the men will clamber down for a quick drink or two.'

'I see,' Walt said morosely. 'Once some of those boys have a few and loosen up, they might not be so eager to leave again.'

'Oh, that's all right. The train can pick them up here in the morning as easily as at Sand Hill. If they just won't leave when they're told, well, all we have to do is roll them out the back door in the direction of the hotel.'

'Which isn't even built yet.'

Diane was briefly thoughtful. 'No, but it will be!' She restored herself with a breath of fresh energy. 'This phase won't last long, Walt. Soon Number Eight will reach Denver and after that happens, we'll have trains running through here every day, in both directions.'

'That's so, and if you're able to get all the carpentry done by them, get some furniture and maybe some gambling tables freighted in, you should be in good shape, then you can move on to your next obvious step, building a town around you.'

'A town?' Diane echoed with a laugh. 'Walt, your lack of business acumen is downright amazing. Why in the world would anyone want to move to a town way out here where there is nothing, can never be anything?'

Walt felt a slow, even thrumming behind his eyes — he was developing the sort of headache Diane always prompted when he talked to her too long.

'There are much better places to be, Walt.'

'I know, and I'd be in one of them myself if I could only get my boss to buy me a horse.' She looked nearly astonished as she always did when Walt told her that he wished to go.

'You'll see,' Diane told him, patting his shoulder. 'Everything will be beautiful, safe and cool once we're finished. Then you won't be in such a rush to take your leave.'

'If everything goes according to plan,' Walt answered.

'Of course it will. Look how far we've

gotten! What could possibly go wrong now?'

Those are words that should never be spoken by anyone. As Diane's sentence trailed off, Walt began to detect the sounds of a hard-running horse at a distance. He turned toward the south, the direction of the sounds and within a minute they saw a lathered gray horse charging down the near side of a forty-foot sand dune, aiming directly toward them.

Diane made a small gasping sound and grabbed Walt's arm as if to lead him toward the front of the saloon but there was no need for that. Walt had been off and striding that way at the first sight of the dark, fleeing man. He had to be fleeing, for no sane man rides that way in that weather, in that country.

'Do you know him?' Walt asked as the rapidly approaching figure shook itself free of the shadows and the haze of distance. Diane only gasped again, tightened her grip on Walt's arm. She did not answer.

It didn't matter, Walt supposed. The man was riding hard, obviously hurt. He would be there in minutes. The rider tilted to one side and then the other as he tried to sit his saddle at a run, indicating to Walt that the man had nearly had it. The incomer's right arm was dangling loosely at his side, his horse was near to stumbling as it slowed itself without the suggestion of the reins. The horse was ready to drop, so was its rider.

The fleeing man, Walt saw, was whiskered, on the near side of thirty, wearing rough range clothing and a broad black hat with a flat crown. His head, as if palsied, shook on his neck and his eyes, wide and very white drifted toward where Diane, trembling throughout her body, stood beside Walt, leaning against him as if for support. Toby had heard the uproar and now emerged from the saloon, still drying a glass on a white cloth.

'Who's that?' Toby asked.

'Don't you know?' Walt said.

'No, why would I?'

'The man has ridden a long way; I figure he could only have come from Sand Hill.'

'I never seen him that I can remember,' Toby said, placing rag and glass aside on an empty whiskey barrel which stood outside the front door with the words painted on it in red: Plenty more inside, boys!

'He's falling!' Diane said excitedly. Yes, he was, but Walt managed to reach the side of the gray horse before the man gave it up completely, sagging toward the ground. With his left hand the rider stretched out, trying to recover his saddlebags but he hadn't the strength.

Walt caught the slumping man across his shoulder. The gray horse stood by, frothing, shuddering. There was little hope for its survival.

'Where should I put him?' Walt asked. From the corner of his eye he could tell that Diane was untying the saddlebags.

Perhaps angry at being caught, she yelled back, 'Inside, for God's sake! At least get him out of the sun!'

'Into the store room,' Toby Riggs said, leading the way. The store room wasn't much to look at — a few cases of beans, sacks of potatoes, whole hams hanging from hooks along the ceiling, but it also had a stack of mattresses due to go upstairs into the rooms if they were ever completed. Toby yanked one of these from the top of the stack and let it drift to the hard wooden floor. They lowered the rider onto the mattress, trying to make it easy for the man who did not look well at all.

Straightening, Toby stood with hands on hips, chest rising and falling with the exertion. He looked pitiably at the wounded man and said to Walt in a low voice, 'It looks as if we might have to start ourselves a graveyard.' It sounded pitiless, but was not meant that way. 'Well, Walt, what are you thinking?'

Walt tipped backed his hat, crouched to touch the dying man's arm and stood again.

'Me,' he said, looking away and out the back door of the store room which opened onto the desert. 'I've been thinking that we've seen what can happen next and wondering how much worse it can get.'

6

There had never been much of a doubt about it and the stranger passed away during the night, never having spoken a word to them. Toby and Walt both watched over the dying man as best they could — it wasn't much without medicine and bandages. Walt doubted if even a surgeon could have helped the man. He was pretty badly shot up.

They gave him a blanket against the chill of night, and water which he seemed to crave but could not easily drink. By four in the morning, the man's body had ceased twitching and his flesh had cooled.

Diane had been watching off and on, but there was nothing she could do either, and if she was hopeful that the man would somehow make it, she was disappointed. They hollowed out a grave for the stranger in the yard.

Diane told them nothing of who the man had been. Toby and Walt had to assume that she knew, simply because Diane seemed to know everything. As the sand drifted over the grave, both it and the man it held became nearly invisible and forgotten.

Walt was sure that Diane had grabbed the dead man's saddlebags, but he saw no point in bothering to bring that up — she would tell him nothing, he knew. For some reason the event prodded him more strongly to get out of there. He thought that this, of all places on the wide spread desert, could become a focus for dying.

The morning after, he led the two horses, Diane's bay and the wobbly gray to the catch basin he had dug in the shallow creek bed. He found Clyde Waring sitting on the sand bank in the quiet shade of the willow trees. He was sketching aimless figures in the white sand with a twig.

'Busy morning?' Walt asked.

'About what you see,' Clyde answered

with a laugh. 'I haven't got anyone to talk to yet. You at least have that.'

'Do I? Diane only talks to me when she has an order.'

'Oh, well, she's just that sort, I guess.' He cleared his throat and lit his pipe again. 'I saw the man who rode in. I don't suppose he made it.'

'No, he didn't,' Walt said as he watched the horses drink. The bay was pushy, crowding the water hole. The lethargic gray, apparently a broken animal, just took it.

Clyde breathed out a plume of blue smoke. The morning sun was bright through the willows. 'I don't suppose you know who owned that horse, do you?'

'No, I don't. I don't suppose we're meant to know.'

'The woman does keep her secrets close,' Clyde said, blowing another stream of smoke. 'You know, don't you, Walt, that the solitary rider we've been seeing for weeks is still out there?'

'I've noticed him. He must be getting

hungry — he broke into our store room a few nights ago.' Well, no one could actually say he *broke* in, since the door still had not been hung on the rear of the saloon.

'You saw him doing it?' Clyde wanted to know.

'Saw him right near,' Walt said as if he didn't particularly care.

'You didn't take a shot at him?'

'No.' Walt shrugged. 'I'm not much for shooting a man just because he's hungry.' He rose then, pushing the bay away from the water. It had had enough and the gray nearly none.

'Going to bring that horse back into shape to make your getaway on?' Clyde asked. It wasn't clear to Walt if the man was kidding or not. It mattered neither way.

'Just trying to keep the poor beast alive for a while. He wouldn't eat his hay earlier, though I had a bucket of water there for him.'

'I saw you.' Clyde nodded. 'A horse like that — you never know. They sometimes come back just out of stubbornness. Their work is to run, and damn all, they'll run their heart out even if they haven't an idea in the world to where they're running.'

'And some men as well.'

'Some men as well,' Clyde agreed. 'I guess I'd better get back to the tank, though I don't have a thing to do.' He dusted off his trousers. 'I guess I'll be seeing you at the barbecue tomorrow.'

'At the . . . ?' Walt turned around sharply.

'That's what Diane has planned. Didn't she tell you?'

'No. She wouldn't. But how in the world does she plan to do that, Clyde?'

'Well, she told me just because they'll be bringing in a trainload of people, and Number Eight will need to have its belly filled.'

'How can . . . does the woman run the damn train line now?'

'You'd have to draw your own conclusions about that. All I know is that she seems to get pretty much what she wants from the Colorado and Eastern — haven't you noticed?'

'I've noticed, but . . .'

'It's the way things are, Walt. Don't hurt your brain trying to figure it out. The woman is purely a mystery.'

A barbecue was what the lady wanted and so a barbecue was what she got. A few of the men brought along their own food, including a couple of nice cuts of beef. A couple more brought their wives and kids. As the sand started to lift on what turned out to be a windy day on the desert, these tired women who had arrived wearing their finery, scooted the disappointed looking children inside where they played made-up games in the store room as their less active fathers practised bending their elbows.

A mob of seven or eight men had remained at the train where they now unloaded furniture including, wonder of wonders, a canopied bed which was immediately taken upstairs where Diane, who had not shown her face downstairs, had it placed and positioned exactly.

Walt heard the idle talk as he wandered across the floor of the saloon. A lot of it was predictable.

'Well, you were wanting to finish off that panel to the wall.'

'We might as well do it today — who knows when we'll be back.'

'Tom's already up on the roof. Said he couldn't stand to see any job he was working on go half-finished.'

'At least we'd be accomplishing. Anybody know where we stored the two by fours?'

Toby, of course, was standing behind the bar which now sported a plank of very dark maple. Walt told him across the bar, 'I guess drinks and food are a good enough reason to turn this she-bang into a work party.'

'You didn't doubt that Diane could turn the men to their trades, did you?'

'No,' Walt had to say, 'but it can't be much fun for you.'

Toby said, 'It's not supposed to be,

94

Walt. Remember I've got a job here as bartender.' With a hint of recrimination, he added, 'Aren't you supposed to be guarding Diane or something instead of wandering around?'

'Toby,' Walt replied, tipping back his hat and resting his forearms on the bar, 'the woman has forty hard-muscled working men around her in this place. If any slippery assassin had an idea of attacking our princess, you can bet he's given it up as a bad job.'

Two men at the other end of the bar were summoning Toby and he walked that way.

Two boys playing tag rushed past, three others in pursuit. Though the sand outside was blowing with some strength, Walt walked past a pair of men sharing glasses of liquor, attending a nice rack of barbecued beef ribs. These looked tasty and could be scented above the sand blow.

'You'll have to build a cook shack next time,' Walt said, holding the flapping brim of his hat back. The men, content with their liquor and day off work, just grinned back.

On Walt's way around the corner of the building, he came upon Diane Kingsley sheltering there, her eyes, squinting because of the sand, turned upward toward the eaves. Above, two men with framing hammers pounded away although the wind was tearing at their clothing.

'They'd never work like that for pay,' Walt commented, startling Diane.

She looked at him with a smile. 'They wouldn't, would they? That's the advantage of having friends.'

And an open whiskey barrel, Walt started to say, but did not.

'Where are you off to?' Diane asked.

'Down to water the horses as long as you don't need any special guarding right now.'

'I thought you delivered it in buckets these days.'

'I usually do. But now and then I like to get out and walk around a little. I think the horses do too.'

'Won't sand have blown in that tank of yours?'

'Probably. I'll take a shovel along. I've been wanting to widen it out anyway.'

Clyde hadn't come over to see him. Probably he was hunkered down in his shack, letting the wind blow. That reminded Walt that he hadn't yet seen the interior of the place. Did Clyde have everything he wanted there? The carpenters couldn't have spent much time spiffing things up after the saloon opened; the bulk of their time was spent at Diane's place.

The door to the station was open three bare inches. The sand-laden wind was buffeting Walt's back as he trudged up to it, nearly losing his hat once. He rapped on the door frame and called out, 'Clyde, are you in there?'

'Come on in, Walt. I'm safe, happy and out of the sand.'

Inside there was a flickering kerosene lantern resting on a low counter, bed on the floor occupied now by Clyde, two wooden chairs looking brand new, a single, narrow striped Indian blanket on the wall and little else.

'Cosy, ain't it?' Clyde asked. 'I guess the railroad is saving lumber. I shouldn't complain; I can at least stand up in here. It's enough for one man alone. What I'll do if I ever get a spider to help out, I can't say.' Clyde's complaints were real enough but he voiced them with humor.

'They still haven't sent you a man?'

'Not unless he's hiding out some-where, or over at the saloon, drinking.'

'No,' Walt said. 'I know most of those men by face now, and I didn't see any strangers around. But that's what I wanted to ask you about, Clyde — why don't you try to snag a few of those carpenters away from there and use them for a quick touch-up in here, if you've a use for them?'

'I couldn't separate them from their seats even using main force. After today it plain won't be possible in no way.'

'Why's that?' Walt frowned.

'Tomorrow's the day. Why do you think Diane wanted to make sure the saloon is all of a piece by then?'

'I'm sorry, Clyde, I still don't take your meaning.'

'Didn't take my meaning! Why, Walt, are you just half-smart or kept rolled up in a carpet of ignorance? Diane is the one who told me. And she sure ought to know — tomorrow is the day the ladies get here.'

Walt Cassidy could only stand with his eyes turned down and his hands curled into half-fists. He had heard Clyde correctly, of that there was no doubt. Knowing Diane as he did, the Monday morning train would be transporting women to work in the saloon. Well, he considered, it had been the next logical step for her to take. How many there were to be, where they could have come from were questions that Clyde would not be able to answer so Walt didn't bother to ask.

He did know one thing, whiskey and women had always and everywhere added up to trouble. If there was ever a time to think quite seriously about getting out of here, it was now.

Walking away from the well station through the sandy heat of the day, he thought that his problems of doing that were the same as ever — he had made no progress at all in the days spent on the desert. Maybe Diane was firmly entrenched here now, her future and her fortune now assured.

Maybe so, but Walt still had no horse, no money. Men came and went but they came only for Diane. The train came and went, but Walt was not wanted on board Number Eight.

At this time the train was only running one way: from where he stood back to Sand Hill where he had a murder warrant on his head for all he knew.

In the saloon yard with the sounds of revelers rising from within, a few adventuresome kids running around outside, he encountered a dour-looking Toby Riggs. The bartender stood in a sliver of shade beneath the narrow gable projecting on this end of the roof.

'How's it going, Toby?' Walt asked, trying for a cheerful mood. Toby looked up but did not smile.

'You've kept that horse alive?' Toby said, looking at the gaunt, miserable sight of the animal.

'Well, he didn't lose that much weight, so there's a chance still.'

'No, maybe he didn't lose that much weight, Walt. But he lost something more important — his heart.' Toby walked to the gray which seemed as if it had collapsed upon itself, and stroked its muzzle.

'He might come out of this all right, despite that run,' Walt said.

'No!' Toby was emphatic about it. 'He won't. You cut the heart out of a beast and it still may live on to wander uselessly around the yard, wanting some meaning to return to his life, even knowing it never will . . . It's not really alive, Walt. Not after what's happened to it.'

101

Needing to change the subject, Walt said, 'Well, I guess you know that some girls are supposed to arrive on the morning train.'

'Yes, I know that,' Toby mumbled. 'I've spent the last hour toting mattresses upstairs from the storeroom.'

Walt thought he detected a slight criticism of himself in Toby's words, but he didn't rise to the bait. Walt had made it clear, and often, that he would confine his duties to the one matter he had been hired on to do and not expand his labors to other areas.

He was a personal bodyguard, that was all.

It did give Walt pause to think . . . 'She'll be needing more help if this all goes as she's planned, with trains from Denver coming through and all, people leaving from Sand Hill, with a flock of girls staying here.'

'Yes,' Toby sighed. They had started away from the saloon to return the two horses to their normal position where the bay stayed by virtue of an anchor and the gray because it needed to be close to the bay horse, having no other friend and no other known place to go to across the wide desert.

'That's only just occurred to you, Walt, but Diane has been thinking about all of these things day and night since the time she determined that building a saloon for herself was necessary. That is the way our Diane is.'

'I suppose so but she's so tight with her information that you'd think it pained her to let loose of any of her secrets.'

Toby paused and then said somewhat apologetically, 'I'm sorry, Walt, I keep forgetting that you didn't know Diane before you found yourself here — that you knew nothing of her problems, her life in Sand Hill. Me, well, if you recall, I didn't much think of talking of those matters. I suppose there'll be time now — Diane has assigned us both sleeping accommodations in the store room. I think Joe Buck and Arnie have even taken some four by fours and nailed together beds for us . . . in between drinks.'

'It'll do,' Walt said, 'for the time being.' He was thoughtful. 'If you know what Diane has in mind, Toby, what about these extra men who are coming in the morning? Where are they going to bed down, and more important, what are their jobs going to be?'

'Well, she told me only because I have to know if I'm going to have to work with them,' Toby said as they started down toward the saloon where, Toby told him, the boss herself was tending the bar.

The wind had died down and the sand put its angry head to rest. All of the children seemed to have escaped from their forced confinement and ran, jumped, whistled and punched their way along the long road toward adulthood. Walt glanced at them, envying them and yet regretting the troubles they would face along the way. No one ever said that passing through life was an easy trek.

'One of the new men, I know, is a relief bartender, for which I'm grateful.'

'And the other?' Walt asked as Toby seemed to falter.

'Just the muscle for the saloon,' Toby said. 'Every such establishment needs a man who's willing to escort the troublemakers out the door.'

'A bouncer.'

'That's it.' Toby looked briefly fearful. 'And this one is one bad man, a mean man, Walt.'

'Then you know him?'

'He worked in the Cock's Crow for a while, but he was so rough he got himself fired. He broke an arm belonging to a friend of the owner there . . .'

'Then Diane didn't own the Cock's Crow?' Walt asked.

'The real owner,' Toby said.

'You're talking about this Captain Pruitt.'

'No, I'm not,' Toby said with a little heat — he wanted to tell the story his way. 'Captain Pruitt didn't get into

Sand Hill until the railroad brought him. As to having money for all I can see, Pruitt is spending the railroad's money and not his own.'

'Seems like it,' Walt agreed. 'All right . . . the bouncer.'

Toby took a deep breath and dabbed at his forehead with his handkerchief. His voice lowered a little as he said, 'You won't like him, Walt. You won't like him a bit. His name is Shannon Pike and he dearly loves to hurt people, to impress them.'

'A man of some size, is he?'

'He's a man of some weight, yes, and most of it seems to be leather and steel strap. Shannon Pike is a fearsome man, Walt. He's a plain thug.'

'But surely Diane knows all of this — why would she hire the man?'

'Is there another candidate?'

'No, but still . . . '

'But still she is going to need a bouncer if the business grows like she is thinking. I don't want the job, Walt — do you?'

Walt Cassidy expelled some air in what might have been a laugh. 'Me? I don't even want the job I have!'

'Yes, well someone is going to have to do the rough work if we start getting larger crowds in.'

'I suppose so,' Walt said.

There was no law in town, no town as a matter of fact and he knew too well what sort of men were roaming around the desert, always prowling, always spoiling for a fight. Once those men got liquored up, they had been known to rip up some real estate. And Diane was crazy enough, or sage enough to have apparently hired some women to work in the saloon. Yes, she was right to expect trouble; she was doing her best to bring it to her. It was Walt's turn to shrug and look across the long sandy desert.

It was a rough time in a rough land; a lot of men who were keeping the peace out here were every bit as bad as the outlaws.

'Besides,' Toby Riggs said, 'Diane

would never abandon one of her own — even a man like Shannon Pike. He did his work as required, just had a tendency in getting a little over zealous in protecting his yard. Still, he did his job — the Cock's Crow is one quiet drinking place most of the time. Diane thought that Pike deserved another chance at a job.'

'Is that what she told you?' Walt asked.

'That, and Pike was the answer to the question I asked you a minute ago — who else is there to take the job that she can count on?'

'Is he riding out here?'

'No, he'll be on the train, just like the women. Old Number Eight doesn't know it, but that morning train is going to be loaded with pure dynamite.'

7

Evening arrived stealthily, with a flourish of color spreading across the empty sky and the empty land as well. Walt Cassidy stood behind the now quiet saloon, watching the changing sky. He wondered if the carpenters had left any of that barbecued beef behind. If so, he would fix himself a plate to eat and then give his new bedroom a try. He found Toby earlier, sitting on a crate, taking a rest from his day's work.

'Well, you're all set for the night, from now on,' Toby said a little sharply.

'What do you mean, Toby? I don't get what you're talking about.'

'What do you think?' he asked, still a little bitterly. 'The carpenters finished up your room for you, made you a bed. I toted the mattress upstairs by myself. Me, I'm stuck in the storeroom.'

'I didn't know anything about that,' Walt said.

'I figured it was some kind of deal you'd made with Diane . . . if you were going to stay on.'

'Well, you were figuring wrong. I am not staying on here. I'm leaving as soon as I can get a horse or the railroad decides I am a real citizen again.'

'That won't be until the line's through to Denver.'

'Then that's when I'm leaving — assuming Diane ever gives me enough cash money to purchase a ticket.'

Toby smiled faintly, 'I'm sorry, Walt. I guess you're not being treated much grander than I am.'

'I'm thinking that maybe when this Shannon Pike gets here, she'll be ready to slip me a few dollars and send me on down the road.'

Toby was shaking his head heavily. 'Nope, that's not the way it will work, Walt. Pike is going to be the saloon bouncer, your job is quite different.' Walt looked at him in the semi-darkness of the store room until Toby clarified his meaning. 'Pike is here to watch the saloon; you're here to protect Diane from men like Shannon Pike. She'll need you both.'

Walt smiled thinly. 'I hadn't thought of it like that . . . ' His head turned around sharply.

He cocked it to one side and held up a hand for Toby to remain silent. Unable to refrain from speaking, the bartender whispered, 'What is it, Walt?'

In a low voice, Walt replied, 'A horse. Didn't you hear it?'

'A horse? Probably you were just wishing you heard one. Who is there to ride around here, and if there was someone, why wouldn't he step into the saloon, no matter who it was?'

'I don't know,' Walt said, moving toward the rear door. 'He's gone now. It could have been one of Diane's millions of friends, but I think you'd better keep your rifle close and sleep lightly.'

Toby went off to do whatever work was required to shut the saloon down for the night and left a vigilant Walt to stand sentry. It might have meant nothing, but on this godforsaken desert where few men passed, Walt believed it did mean something. The flurry of recent activity may have drawn someone's attention to them, and the night rider could have been a scout sent to investigate. He thought of asking Diane Kingsley, but she would never tell him if she did have an inkling.

Walt wondered idly if this rider could have been pursuing the dead man who had ridden in. He also wondered again what was in the saddlebags Diane had lifted from the dead man's horse. He knew he had no chance of finding that out, either.

Stomach full of barbecued beef and homemade bread, he climbed the new staircase to the second storey. There was only moonlight to see by, but the moon was full and leaked in to polish the freshly cut pine planks. The hallway was empty, of course, and at the head of the corridor a door stood open. Someone had thrown his saddle onto the floor of the new-made room. The window was unglazed, but Walt wandered that way and stood before it, watching the long desert change colors, its shadows shift beneath the clouded moonlight. He had unbuttoned his shirt and bent to see to his boots when he again heard a familiar but stealthy sound. Someone on horseback was prowling the land.

He at first took the horseman to be the lone rider who haunted the vicinity, but whose only trespass to date had been to search for water and food. It was not.

They were trying to arrive with stealth, but one by one Walt was able to pick out the figures of four different horsemen as they guided their ponies over the sea of sand toward the saloon. Again, he thought first of lawmen, but these men had a different sort of air about them. None wore a badge that was visible by the moonlight, that was for sure.

Long experience in open country had

taught Walt that out here, every man was an enemy until he proved himself to be a friend. Friends did not prowl the night and reaching for his hat, Walt went out again into the corridor and headed for the stairs, pistol in his hand.

It seemed that it was time for him to begin earning his keep.

The steps down were a descent into the deeper gloom of the saloon. He thought he heard someone's mount blow outside, but could not be sure. His senses were on such high alert that he found he could not trust them. Solid forms could not be distinguished from shadows, each sound seemed to have ominous undertones.

Pausing at the foot of the stairs, he let his eyes search the windows across the sawdust-littered floor. His boot steps seemed loud and clumsy. 'Face it, Walt, you've got a bad case of nerves,' he told himself.

Well, he had the right to them. Alone, cornered on the broad desert by a band of unknown searching men, with no

114

help to call on except for Toby Riggs and Clyde Waring, neither of whom were the type to stand up to armed raiders in a night fight. It was the worst spot Walt had been in for a long while, since that long-ago day down in Palos Verde when . . .

The crack of splintering wood brought Walt sharply from his reverie. That was the front door which as he knew had only been fitted with a small flimsy lock. He dove aside, drawing his Colt as he rolled into the legs of a table. It was a good thing he had, for as he was pulled up sharply by the table legs, twin stabs of flames flared in the night, accompanied by the bellow of a large-gauge shotgun. The intruder had fired both barrels at once in his haste, leading Walt to believe he had time to steady himself and return fire while the night bandit reloaded.

He had started to rise, that thought having passed quickly through his mind when from the corner of his eye, he saw the bulky figure at the window behind him. Walt ducked again, shifting his sights as he did.

Three rapidly fired rifle shots from the window punched through the top of the table, leaving porcupine sprays of splinters hanging down. Walt pushed the table onto its side, coming up behind it, then he cut loose with the thunder of his Colt. Flame painted bright patterns against the wall; the gun bucked repeatedly in his hand and the man who had been reaching across the sill for a hand-hold looked at Walt with blank astonishment and then toppled head-first into the saloon to lie sprawled against the floor.

He hadn't forgotten the man with the shotgun, far from it, but his fight had to be held on one front at a time. Now as he spun back around, seated now against the floor, he saw a wide figure of a man standing menacingly in the doorway.

'Hey, you!' a voice called from the foot of the stairs and Walt shifted his eyes to see Diane in a sheer yellow nightdress. 'I won't have this in here! Get out of here, you've caused enough trouble!' She held a chrome, purse-sized revolver in her hand. The man with the shotgun seemed to shrug off any concerns he might have had about killing a woman and shouldered his weapon. A pistol shot cracked immediately through the room and Walt saw the bad man slap at his forehead and then crumple up where he stood, the shotgun clattering to the floor.

Walt glanced first at Diane who seemed not to have fired. Slowly the small dark figure of Toby Riggs emerged from the shadows of the store room.

'Well,' he said a little shakily, 'I got him.' He looked toward Diane as if hoping for some show of gratitude, but the stolid woman remained stolid.

'Who are they?' she asked Walt Cassidy.

'Don't ask me. I'm not from around here, remember?'

'I think I've seen this one,' Toby said,

117

creeping forward to look at the body of the man he had shot. 'His name escapes me.' His eyes lifted to Diane's. 'He used to ride with Ray John Pettit.'

Diane's face showed no expression, but it was the sort of expressionlessness that someone is working hard to present — tight and unconvincing.

'Well, what's done is done. You boys bury these two before you go to bed, will you? It's a good thing Shannon Pike and the girls are coming in on the morning train.'

'Yeah,' Walt said peevishly, 'we need nothing but a gun hand and a few saloon girls to calm things down.'

Diane continued on her way as if she had not heard him. Reaching the bottom of the step, she gripped the banister, smiled meaninglessly at both of them and ascended in a swirl of chiffon.

Toby Riggs said, 'If this keeps up, we're going to have to hire another man just to tend the graveyard we keep for passersby.'

'Tell me, Toby, is this Shannon Pike the kind who shoots first and ask questions later?'

Toby answered quite seriously, 'I've never heard Shannon Pike ask any questions at all.'

'Like that, is he?'

'Like that.'

'Toby, you are going to have some interesting times here.'

'And you?'

'I'm leaving as soon as I can find a way.'

'That probably won't be until the Denver trains start running regular — if they'll even agree to sell you a ticket.'

'I know that, Toby, but that's not what I had in mind. These two unknown bundles of meat on our floor rode in here on some kind of animals. When we're done removing them, I'm going horse hunting.'

They had bent to hoist the first dead man and carry him toward the store room door when the door snapped open again and the wild-eyed man with a rifle in hand burst into the room.

'I see I'm too late,' said a disheveled Clyde Waring. His thin hair was mussed; he was only half-dressed. He lowered his rifle. 'I saw them, you know, but by the time I got my boots tied it was all over.' He looked at both dead men. 'What did they want?'

'Whiskey is my first guess,' Walt said. 'It's not that easily come by out here, and there was one man by earlier while the carpenters were still here drinking it up. Might have given them the idea.'

'That must be it,' Clyde agreed, looking around the room. 'I knew those railroad carpenters were quick, but it's a wonder how fast this place is coming together.'

'When are they going to string wire?' Toby asked. Walt looked at the smaller man with a frown of interest. Toby explained, 'They'll string telegraph wire soon; they have to, it's in all their contracts.'

'That's right,' Clyde said, 'by the end of the week that shack of mine will be a hub of the country. I've got a book they sent me to study Morse code. 'Slow but easy, Clyde,' was what they advised. 'You can learn it that way.''

'That sounds fine.'

Clyde laughed. 'I don't expect to get more than a message or two a week. The rest of the hum will be through chatter to Denver. But I'm going to learn to use a telegraph key if it kills me. One day, maybe, I'll have me an office in some small town. Meanwhile I'm using the thing to practice on every day — requesting a spider!'

'You could still be of help to us if you've a mind, Clyde.' Toby tilted his head toward the two bodies. The tank boss let out a heavy sigh, but agreed.

'It's not my favorite kind of work, boys, but I'll do it.' He asked Toby, 'Maybe I could get a little nip of whiskey to help me through this arduous task?'

'All right. I'll hit the barrel; I think I could use a drink myself. Walt?'

'None for me.'

Toby scuttled away behind the bar.

'Clyde — did you see those men ride away?' Walt wanted to know.

'I did. They grabbed the reins to their partners' horses and spun off toward the open desert.'

Walt groaned inwardly. He had almost come to believe rescue was at hand. But horses were as scarce and more valuable than whiskey on the desert — he should have known the other night riders would not leave them behind.

Toby noticed Walt's expression. 'What's wrong, Walt?'

'Nothing,' he answered with a burdened voice. 'It's just that it seems I'm doomed to live out my life in this desolate saloon. Let's bury the dead, boys, and pay me no mind if I jump in after them.'

As they worked in the silent grayness of the moon-shadowed night, spades dipping into sand, two silent dead men with their arms crossed, waiting for the nestling earth, Walt spoke to Clyde

Waring who was making hard work of the digging.

'Who is Ray John Pettit, Clyde?'

'Ray John! Don't tell me he's around?' Clyde asked. The news seemed to be enough to cause him to hesitate and stagger a bit.

'Toby says he thinks one of these men was a Ray John Pettit rider.'

'Well, he might know, having worked at the Cock's Crow. I never seen him, Ray John never had no taste for the kind of liquid supplies I got, unless maybe to water his horse.' Clyde rested on his shovel.

'Who he is, is one mean man, Walt, and one of the most successful at it. I thought you would have heard the name even way down in Los Gatos. What Ray John is, is a cattle thief, a bank robber and a killer, the leader of twenty men who are all accustomed to firing their guns at the first opportunity. And you have picked a fight with him.'

Walt himself paused in his works, looking up to the night sky. Could he possibly get himself in any deeper trouble? Toby Riggs who had stopped a moment himself to listen, cracked a joke which was in no way funny, but broke the tension.

'Well, at least we have Shannon Pike on our side, and he's no less of a bastard.'

8

The now-familiar form of the Number Eight locomotive appeared in the distance, seeming tiny as it waded through the steel-gray of the ground fog. Its whistle blared once, piercingly and in a matter of minutes, Clyde Waring was on the porch of his small home, wiping back his hair to plant his gray striped railroad cap. Clyde stood there, hands on hips, waiting. His mouth was a little tight — he still did not think that a man of his age and experience should be subjected to climbing the ladder of the water tank.

Diane had emerged from the saloon into the cool morning light, wearing some sort of blue gingham dress which was unusual for her, she being partial to finery. She folded her arms and leaned against one of the uprights on the saloon's front porch, watching the train labor its way up Grade Forty-Four toward them.

On this morning, Walt had a new shave, a clean white shirt and stiff new pair of blue jeans. Once Diane made a promise you could count on it coming true, and she had vowed he would have clean clothes and a shave. On this morning, she had promised to deliver some dance hall girls and the less-than-famous, quite nasty Shannon Pike. There was no telling what or who else she had ordered, but there was bound to be some surprise on the Number Eight.

Long shadows and the swish of gingham preceded Diane as she moved toward Walt, who could already make out the circled eight on the locomotive's chest as the iron horse proceeded in their direction. She spoke to him quickly, breathily.

'Walt, after last night, it seems we could use a marshal. Would you consider taking the job?' She took his arm as she spoke. Walt didn't laugh out loud, but he came close.

He told his benefactor, 'Diane, we haven't even got a town, no citizens, no jail, marshal's office, and no laws and no courts. Besides, I have a job, remember? Ask Toby there if he'd consider.'

'I'd have to get a badge cut in half,' she said, even though the diminutive Toby Riggs was in range of hearing. Her interest shifted to the arriving train. 'Well, here they are! Now we can get this operation rolling.' She rubbed her hands together eagerly and started toward the smoking, clanking locomotive as it spewed out jets of braking steam.

'What's up now?' Toby Riggs asked, apparently having gotten over his hurt feelings. Walt doubted that there was any way Diane, his goddess, could have injured him for long. The little bartender made a pathetic figure, and Walt was only happy that it was not him on the goddess's altar.

'I'm just waiting to see. We know that

Diane will have at least one surprise for us.'

It was no surprise when at least half of the railroad workers slid down to the ground and headed straight for the saloon.

'I've gotta go,' Toby said and darted that way himself.

The man in the dark suit and derby hat was no surprise when he slid from the freight car, either. He was a stranger to Walt, but his kind was not. Shannon Pike had a round, closely-clipped head, a slightly flat face with a small broken nose and a scar in his right eyebrow. He wore a narrow mustache which was uneven due to the scars on his upper lip. His hands were large with oft-broken knuckles. He had a barrel chest, long, ape-like arms and tiny, almost feverish dark eyes.

Walt disliked the man immediately; Diane went to Pike, welcoming him warmly, though she kept an eye on Walt as the two hugged. The gesture meant different things to each of those two, that was obvious. Pike's eyes glittered and he smiled crookedly as Diane's wandering eye slid away from Pike.

'Ah, here they are!' she said, making her escape from Pike's arms. To Walt she said, 'Aren't things going well?'

'Just fine,' he answered, drawing a scowl from Pike, apparently yet another friend of Diane's who could stand no potential romantic rival. Walt could have told the man he didn't have to worry about that. Walt had no intention of ever buying a ticket for that particular merry-go-round.

A sharp whistle went up from one of the freight cars, and as Walt watched, three passengers wearing skirts were helped down, whistled at and surveyed appreciatively. Walt turned to start away — the scene revealed too much of what men really were if their reins weren't kept tight. The three skirted figures had started a silent throb pulsing through the crowd. Walt understood the woman-hungry lonely men, but he didn't wish to be identified with them. He had taken three steps when Diane called out, 'Walt, someone has to help these girls with their baggage.'

There were at least twenty men eager to do just that, but Diane explained with smiling patience to these crushed volunteers, 'Sorry, boys, but it has to be an employee of the dance hall. The ladies need their luggage taken upstairs to their rooms and I can't allow anyone but a house man up there. When you return from work and the ladies have had a chance to rest up, I'm sure they'll be happy to spend a little time with each of you.'

Dance hall, was it now?

Oh, well, it was Diane's place, she could call it whatever she wanted. Walt supposed that having three female employees raised the status of the saloon in her mind. But she could have taken on one or two of the friendly known railroad men to give Walt a hand with what seemed to be a mountain of cases and trunks. One thing was sure:

unlike Walt, these girls were not planning on leaving anytime soon.

Below, three or four men stood on the porch drinking their morning whiskey, watching the new arrivals and apparently enjoying seeing the unhappy Walt actually do some work. The bell on the Number Eight rang three times and the railroad workers slammed down their drinks and sprinted toward the train.

Diane and Clyde Waring were right, this water stop required more than an hour. However, the train's schedule makers had not designed it that way — there was work to be done. Number Eight was rolled forward to the water tank where Clyde could be seen scaling the ladder unenthusiastically. Walt had to admit he saw Clyde's point — climbing up and down the twenty-five foot ladder twice daily, wrestling the heavy filler spout into position and locking it away were not the sort of jobs a man approaching sixty — which Walt took Clyde to be — was likely to find easy.

He had seen Clyde earlier, shading his eyes as he looked toward the train, vainly keeping watch for his expected 'spider'. It seemed that Clyde would have to spend another day practising his telegraphy, asking for his assistant on the wire.

Just as Number Eight began to pull out for its long draw onto the desert, giving an extra blast on the whistle which brought men boiling out of the saloon — some finishing their drinks on the run — a dapper little fellow in a town suit, Irish by his face, slipped out of the locomotive cab itself to land with a plunk against the sandy yard and rise, dusting himself off, picking up his brown derby hat and smiling broadly. A red and black carpetbag was tossed down and the cheerful man picked it up, waving to the men on the train. He strode directly toward Walt, asking, 'Do you know Toby Riggs?'

'There aren't many strangers around here. He's inside.'

'We've got a bit of labor out here, is

why I ask. Jack Green's the name, by the way. I'm Toby's relief bartender.' He thrust out a red hand and Walt shook it.

'A bit of work?' Walt asked, looking toward the tracks where a new addition sat in all its glory. The polished oak bar rested in three sections against the sand. Talking to Diane, Walt had not seen it unloaded. It was decorated with brass, and a nearby wrapped packet had to be a brass foot rail. It would take all of the men they could muster to haul that inside the saloon, and they had no one whose specific job that was.

'How in the world did she manage that?' Walt, who had seen Diane's almost magical acquiring at work before, asked in a low voice.

'I couldn't say, but there it is,' Green said, picking up his carpetbag. 'I'd better find Toby and get settled in.'

'Don't you want to wait and help us with this monster?' Walt asked, nodding toward the heavy bar sections.

'I was told there'd be plenty of help with that,' Jack Green said with a smile.

He tilted his derby and started on.

'Plenty of help . . . ?' Then Walt saw half a dozen carpenters exit the saloon, apparently having missed taking the Number Eight to the job site on purpose.

Tug Travis would be raising hell with someone for this. Somehow Walt did not think Diane Kingsley would be one of those accused.

'There it is, boys!' a workman Walt recognized, Joe Buck, called out, pointing a finger at the bar sections.

'That!' another worker answered. 'That's no more than half an hour's work. Let's get it arranged. I'm anxious to see if my boot fits that bar rail.'

'Tug Travis is going to blister us with his tongue — might even fire a couple of us to prove he means business.'

'You worry too much, Willie. Me, I plan to be so drunk when the evening train rolls in that I won't give a damn what Tug Travis does. If he fires me, well, we're only two days out of

Denver now. I guess I can risk losing two days' pay.'

'I wish now I'd gone with the work train.'

'Well, you didn't. No sense worrying about it now; let's take care of what we can do. After all, we're working on two free rounds of whiskey.'

Was that the going rate for carpenters around here now? He himself got back to the ladies' luggage. Two of them were standing on the front porch, eyeing him impatiently. Walt gave each of the two a cursory appraisal. Both were hovering around the age of thirty, he thought. They were dressed pretty much in the same fashion, the taller darker one with the sharpest eyes in pink. The shorter brunette with the bland face in a deep red get-up. The taller one had a slender, interesting figure, but there was nothing interesting about her eyes or mouth. She followed Walt with the sort of interest a bird has for a beetle. The other just tried to be invisible.

'What rooms did they tell you were yours?' Walt asked.

The tall dark one snapped, 'How would we know? Aren't you the one who should tell us?'

'Maybe, but I can't. I don't know.' Walt put one of the heavier leather satchels down.

'Move along, can't you?' the woman said sharply. 'It's hot out here and we've had a long ride.'

Walt's mouth tightened so that he couldn't tell the woman what he thought of her troubles. To be fair to Diane, she had a dozen problems going on this morning, but she should at least have told Walt where the ladies were to sleep.

'Well?' the sharp voice of the tall woman snapped again.

Walt replied very carefully, 'I at least have to know where I'm carrying them so I don't end up moving them again later. I'll have to ask Diane,' Walt said, setting the other suitcase down.

'You should already know that!' the

woman shrieked.

'Yes, I agree, but I don't. You see, lady,' he said looking at her levelly in a way which ensured they were not going to be friends, 'this is my first day at being a porter for a demanding . . . well, you know what you are.'

The tall woman's eyes popped out of her head and her mouth tightened as her face flushed crimson. 'I'll have you fired, mister! See if I don't.'

'Better and better,' Walt said as he pushed past the other meek, pasty-faced girl. 'Let me know when you've done that, won't you? I think I will have my first drink now.'

She made a sound, much like steam escaping from the train's by-valves as he left the two women there to fume and complain, and made his way to the bar.

Jack Green was already working there, apron around his waist, coatless, grinning.

'What'll it be?' he asked, wiping the top of the new bar in front of Walt.

'Is there a choice?' Walt asked with surprise.

'Sure is. Five barrels of beer were just rolled down that hill. It's bound to make the brew a bit frothy, but if you prefer I can draw you a mug.'

'I'll try it,' Walt said as if he were volunteering. 'It can only get warmer from here on out.' He wondered how Diane had managed to come by beer, but dropped the questioning thought immediately — she would never tell him flat out. She just promenaded along her way, making magic.

The beer was all it could be expected to be — warm, flat but not bad tasting. Walt was finishing his mug when Diane hove into view again. She slid up beside him at the bar and said, 'Luggage, Walt.' She looked appealing, but a little tense on this morning. Probably she had more worries that she let show.

'I didn't like that woman,' Walt said, drinking the last of the foam from the mug.

'I know that. Celia is lucky you didn't

138

slap her. She was raised to be tough in a tough world — I know you can understand that. But we've got to get those women tucked away in their rooms.'

'I didn't know which were theirs.'

She nodded. 'I tacked cards with their names on them to the doors. I'll get one of these guys to paint numbers on them later.' She lifted her chin toward the string of four or five remaining trainmen along the bar.

'They're making good use of their time off.'

'Leave them alone. They brought the bar in and put it together, didn't they, and they rolled the beer down from the train. They now just want to stand around, hoping for a look at my girls. That will be a while. I want them all rested. That means getting them to their rooms,' she said with some emphasis. 'Toby is going to take Celia's trunk and bags up. The thin one. So you don't have to worry about her. Lynn, the other girl — the other one you met on the porch — won't give you any trouble, she never does.'

'I thought there were three of them.' Walt looked around.

'I brought Rowena along,' Diane said. 'She has the room next to yours. You'll have to look around for her.'

'What do you mean?'

'She'll probably be hiding someplace, crying. You'll find her. There aren't many places to hide. You might try the store room first.'

'But . . . ?' With what she had said, Diane turned and was gone, Walt watching after her.

He was left to consider — who was this Rowena; why did she hide; what was behind her tears? He knew that Diane would not answer his questions, so he went off searching for the girl. Toby passed, laden down with luggage, closely followed by the stony-faced Celia who seemed to be herding the bartender. A switch would not have been out of place in the picture. Toby shot an unhappy glance at Walt and continued up the staircase.

Time to find Rowena, Walt decided.

It didn't take much looking. The small blond in the yellow dress with white trim sat on a nail keg in the store room, a white and yellow handkerchief to her nose. Her eyes were red and swollen. She had been crying for a long time.

'You ready to go up to your room now?' Walt asked.

'Who are you?' she asked, looking up with startled eyes. Her blond hair was almost white in the sunlight which fell through the back door. Her nose was very nice, Walt considered, and her blue eyes . . . he shook away his appraising thoughts. He was here for one reason.

'My name's Walt. I need you to show me which luggage is yours. Diane wants you girls tucked away so you can rest.'

'You know where my room is?' she asked in a cautious tone.

'I do. It's not much; the carpenters really haven't finished with it yet.'

He realized that she was not listening

to him. She rose, still crying. She did not sob or shudder, but tears continued to stream down her face. He didn't figure that she would appreciate him asking what her trouble was.

They found her luggage and Walt carried and dragged it along, once passing Toby who nearly smirked at him. Folks seemed to think the sight of Walt working around here was a knee slapping event. Well, he was just doing what his job required. Now, if Diane ever wanted to start paying him extra for extra work . . .

But she hadn't paid him one red cent yet, had she?

He got Rowena into her room. The girl looked around once and then sagged onto her bed where she sat with her face in her hands, crying. He went out feeling angry and embarrassed at once. Why? What did it have to do with him? Let her cry all she wanted.

'Let me have a look at this one!' the rough voice said and Walt came face to face with Shannon Pike. The cruel-looking bouncer had stopped somewhere to comb his hair back with water. It did nothing to make him look more civilized. Just now he was reaching for Rowena's door.

'You don't need to look,' Walt Cassidy said, keeping his place before the door.

Pike's face grew even harder yet.

'You don't tell me what I need to do,' he growled.

'Only as far as watching out for the women — that's my job, remember?'

'Your job is to watch out for Diane — she told me,' Pike insisted, still moving forward.

'And her girls,' Walt insisted, although he had been told nothing of the sort.

Pike stopped, looking like a dazed and confused bull. 'Don't you know who I am?'

'Yes, you're the town bully in Sand Hill, the way I hear it.'

'I broke the arms of the last man

who talked to me like that,' Pike said to Walt.

'Did you?' Walt asked quietly. 'You're from Sand Hill. Did you ever meet a man named Vance Hereford down there?'

Pike's eyes narrowed but his angry expression did not seem to alter. 'Heard of him? I saw him gunned down on a street corner for killing a man's horse.'

Now Pike's bullying glower did seem to alter as he studied Walt more closely. The bouncer now nodded and turned a quarter away. 'Yeah, I guess I know who you are.

'If Diane says so, I guess I won't buck you on this one,' he added quickly, 'but don't get the idea that you're in charge around here!'

Then, satisfied with having had the last bark, Shannon Pike started away toward the head of the stairs, his boots racketing heavily. Surprising Walt, the door at his back opened three inches or so, and, turning his head, he saw the washed-out face of Rowena, one blue eye peering out.

'Thank you,' she whispered. 'Can I ask you something?' Puzzled, Walt nodded and the door was swung open widely enough for him to enter. Some of Rowena's cases had been opened, clothes thrown out and distributed across the room but not as if they were part of a particular plan. Walt thought that she had removed them simply to be doing something. Rowena looked around at the empty room, flushed and said, 'I'm sorry I can't offer you a chair.'

'Not if you don't have one, no. I'll bring up one from downstairs in a while.' Walt looked at the blonde girl who had now stopped crying. Her steady blue eyes met his. 'The chair's not what you wanted to ask me about, is it?'

'No, but one would be appreciated,' Rowena said, retreating to the bed where she sagged down to sit, her folded hands between her knees. 'Is this the end of the line?' she blurted out.

It took Walt a moment to reply.

'No, not actually. They're about forty miles on now, and in two days, I'm told, they'll have the line extended into Denver.'

Rowena's sad eyes were looking up as if they could penetrate the ceiling, or wished to. 'Denver. And what do they have in Denver? A lot of saloons, I suppose.'

Walt said, 'I haven't been there, but I imagine so.'

'A whole lot of saloons with a lot of girls working there,' Rowena said. 'Everyone getting rich . . . like I said, this is the end of the line.' She looked directly at Walt. Her expression might have been considered a smile, but it was a weary one.

'I don't get you,' Walt said. He sat beside her on the bed without having been asked.

'You know, there really is no such thing as the end of the line,' he told her. 'The end is the beginning of a trip for others.'

146

'Like you, Walt?' Rowena asked.

He patted her hand and stood. 'Just like me. When it's time to leave, I'll get up and go — you can count on it.'

He started to say more. It seemed she had still other questions for which he had no answers, so he turned and went out, closing the door gently behind him. The soft crying began again immediately, so he just closed his own door and tramped down the stairs into the saloon. Only Jack Green was there, aimlessly wiping the bar, and two carpenters sitting together at the end of the bar. Walt thought one of the men was asleep. Rather than let Pike say anything to them, he walked up to the trainman who was awake.

'Boys, there's two spare mattresses in the storeroom if you need a rest.'

'Thanks, Walt,' said the man whose name Walt could not remember. 'We won't bother anybody; we'll be gone with the evening train for Sand Hill.'

'Good luck to you,' Walt said. Then,

not wanting to prolong the conversation, he started for the front door which was closed but unlocked.

Outside, it was startlingly bright at this noon hour, hot and sandy — the wind had begun to stir again. All he had to do on this afternoon was bring down a few buckets of water for his herd of two horses. He considered taking them down to the creek which involved less labor unless the hollow had filled in again.

Still considering, he glanced toward the water tower and was amazed to see a tall sorrel horse, unsaddled, standing in the shade behind the tower crew's quarters. Walt started that way, tugging his hat down against the blowing sand, checking that his Colt was loose in its holster. Did that horse signal trouble?

Walt walked to the open door of the shack, keeping his eyes down against the blowing sand, his Colt firmly in his hand. Too many things were going on around here in a place where nothing should be happening. He nudged the door to the cabin open and swung in with his pistol at the level.

A very young blond man was crouched behind the counter where the newly acquired telegraph key and receiver rested. The boy looked up, his pale eyes startled.

'Don't shoot me, mister,' he squeaked.

'I have no wish to, but tell me, where is . . . ?'

Clyde Waring chose to enter at that moment from the outside. He glanced at the startled kid and then at Walt whose hand was still wrapped around his gun butt. 'For God's sake, Walt! What are you doing?'

'Who's this?' Walt asked, waving his gun at the kid.

'Why, this is Danny McElroy — put that Colt away, will you? — he's the spider I've been waiting for.'

Feeling a little sheepish, Walt holstered his pistol. 'Sorry, Mr McElroy,' he said to the young man. 'We've had a little bit of trouble around here lately, and when I saw the strange horse, I thought Clyde here might be in trouble.'

'That's my horse,' Danny McElroy said, straightening up, 'and I promise you I have no intention of causing any trouble.'

'Sorry,' he glanced at Clyde, 'I guess the raid made me a little jittery. Did you tell Danny about it?'

'Hasn't been time, Walt. The man just stepped off the train.'

'I didn't see anyone get off beyond the usual, except for Jack Green — he's another bartender Diane sent for — and I would sure have noticed a man with a horse.'

'He got off on the other side,' Clyde said, now looking at Walt with a sad, slightly contemptuous expression. 'Those Ray John Pettit riders really got you rattled, didn't they, Walt?'

'Ray John Pettit,' Danny McElroy asked, 'is that who it was?'

'Pettit himself wasn't with them but Toby, our bartender, said he knew one of them to be a Pettit man.'

'You ran them off?' the kid continued, interested.

'Shot two of them dead,' Walt admitted, without either pride or shame.

'That's bad, isn't it?' Danny commented.

'That we got two of them?'

'Why, sure,' the kid pointed out. 'You know now that Pettit is camped not far from here; he won't like it that he lost two fighting men. Pettit is said to have more than twenty men riding with him. Men who have been camped out on the desert without much water, little food, no whiskey or — '

'Women,' Walt said. 'We have those, too.'

'He'll be back,' Danny said with a long face. 'It wouldn't take much for Ray John to take all your whiskey and the women, leaving the saloon a pile of ashes smoldering against the desert sky. He's that kind of man.'

'I've heard that he's worse than any

Apache raider,' Clyde put in. 'Well, Danny, now that you've gotten here, I couldn't blame you if you decided to ride right out again.'

Danny McElroy grinned and stretched his arms overhead. 'I think, Clyde, that you had better take me up to the tank once more to make sure I know what I'm doing. When that evening train backs in, I intend to do the job on my own.'

'That's my boy!' Clyde said, quite pleased with the answer. 'It looks like the railroad company finally sent me the right man for the job.'

'Looks like,' Walt agreed. He wasn't really so sure, as far as he could recall the only doors where ramps for unloading a horse could be placed were all along this side of the train, not on the opposite as Danny McElroy had claimed. What did a man need a horse for out here, anyway? If his name was not Walt Cassidy.

And if McElroy was not who he claimed to be, who was he, where had he come from and what new trouble had the blond man carried here with him?

9

Rowena was dressed in ill-fitting jeans and a dark blue shirt when she accompanied Walt to the water hole the next day. Diane had seen them go, leading the bay and the injured gray horse, but she had said nothing. Perhaps she had decided that things were not 'that way' between them or even if they were, there was nothing anyone could do to stop it.

Rowena was cheerful on this morning, showing a new face to the world and to Walt Cassidy. She showed extreme patience as she guided the gray over a rocky patch of ground.

Walt guessed the old boy, having been ridden into the ground, could not be saved. And what had that mysterious rider delivered to Diane on that night? Only one item made any sense. It seemed it was just another matter of a life for gold.

The watering hole needed to be dug out, but it was only half an hour's work and the morning was still cool. Rowena sat in the shade of a clump of thorny mesquites, watching Walt at work, studying the stream as it flowed along through the brush, making its way along on its short life above ground.

They had startled a covey of quail on their arrival. These had now settled again and made their way along the ground to chitter to each other among the brush.

'This isn't such a bad place,' Rowena said. She had walked closer to where Walt finished digging his small catch basin which the horses approached eagerly.

'Yes, it is,' Walt countered. 'There's sidewinders around — I've seen their tracks. There's the warm sun which will be blazing at midday, blistering any exposed flesh. There are tarantulas, scorpions, centipedes along the ground. Worst of all is that if a man leaves his watering hole, there is no telling if he will ever find another or how long it will take. Many have died in their wandering search for water, for life.'

'Like you?' Rowena asked surprisingly. Walt gave it a moment's thought, then smiled and said, 'Maybe so. Maybe a part of me is like a desert rat taunted by the small creatures around, fearing the larger beasts while I search for the next habitable place to settle.'

They had returned to the shade while the horses drank. Rowena smiled again, but it seemed weighted down by past memories or future fears — or both. 'You mentioned larger beasts,' she said thoughtfully.

'Oh, yes,' Walt said, watching a stream of red ants pass across the white sand. 'Coyotes mostly. One will never attack a man, but get enough of them together, and here and there a puma, peccaries who are fearsome when they hunt together, even a bear or two up in the low hills.' Walt glanced at her. 'It's a nasty place to live. To try to. The thirst, the isolation, the loneliness . . . it all might look lovely in a framed painting. It's not.'

'You're here,' Rowena said, sketching figures in the sand with a twig. Her almost-white hair gleamed in the sun and the narrow creek glittered and chuckled as it passed. A light morning breeze had risen.

'I'm passing across it,' Walt said.

'Looking for your next watering hole?' Rowena asked.

'Something like that, I guess.'

'Enduring the small annoyances while staying away of the larger menace.'

'I suppose.' There *were* still other large menaces out there — like Ray John Pettit and his twenty outlaws, like the law in Sand Hill with a hanging noose just his size waiting for him. 'What are you, Rowena, some kind of poet? The way you look at things . . . '

'I can't bring two rhyming words together,' she answered with a hint of sadness.

'Then what are you? What were you, what do you intend to be?'

'I'm only a lone desert traveler,' Rowena said as if with regret.

The bay horse gave the crippled gray an unnecessary head butt and Walt got up to pull the mare away from the water. The bay wanted all of the water although she could not possibly have drunk it.

Walt walked slowly back and settled on the sand again, watching for the ants. After another quiet minute, Walt asked Rowena, 'What happened back in Sand Hill, Rowena?'

'To me? To Diane? What do you mean?'

'All right, then, let's start with you if you don't mind talking about it.'

Rowena sighed and looked directly into Walt's eyes.

'I don't mind, though it's as tiresome to do so as it was to experience it.' She began with a question. 'I suppose you like women, don't you, Walt?'

He nodded, wary of the question.

Rowena went ahead. 'How would you like to be around them all of the time? Fifty of them all wanting your attention, shouting at you, grabbing at you, no matter that you were trying to work?'

'Well . . .'

'No need in coming up with an answer — I know that you wouldn't like it.'

'No, I wouldn't,' he agreed. 'Sounds tiresome.'

'Sure is. Some of those men were even starting to think they had a claim on me because I'd smiled at them a time or two. They didn't understand that was a part of my job, smiling until my mouth hurt. Someone pinched me, I smiled; poked at me, I smiled.'

'Tough, I guess,' Walt considered.

'Well, the job is to make every one of them feel like he is special — that's what they want.'

'I s'pose.' Walt had taken his turn at drawing figures in the sand. He asked at last, 'What was the reason behind

Diane coming out here and starting a saloon where it could never prosper? It makes no sense to me, no matter which way I turn it.'

'She never told you? Well, Walt, I was outside of the dealings so I couldn't vouch for everything I believe I do know.'

She began her story.

'The Cock's Crow was taken over a few years ago by two businessmen named Art Sanders and Lawrence Pettigrew for debts they had, owing from the original owner, a man named David McElroy. Some say it was a swindle — I wouldn't know.

'Anyway,' she said, slapping a mosquito which had landed on her freckled arm, 'it seems that Diane, as manager, had a deal where she was supposed to draw some percentage of the saloon's revenue as her pay. I heard twenty per cent, up as high as fifty per cent. I wouldn't know, but it was a lot of money as you can imagine.'

'Yes, I can. Cock's Crow was always busy.'

Rowena, her legs crossed under her, scooted forward, looking around as if anyone could possibly be near enough around to hear her. 'The thing that happened is that Sanders and Pettigrew got greedy. They couldn't see a need for such an expensive manager; they figured they could do that part themselves and save a huge salary.'

'They let Diane go.' Walt nodded.

'Practically pushed her out the door. She didn't say anything — Diane's not the sort to fuss and wail.'

'But she is the sort to plan,' Walt said, beginning to see a bit of it all.

'She was near me and a couple of other girls who had gone to see her off. She was packing her suitcase when she looked at each of us and said, 'I hope you girls can all find a new home, because I am going to gut the Cock's Crow, no matter what it takes. It might not be mine anymore, but I'm not

161

going to let it be theirs — you can count on it.'

'She didn't say that in an angry voice, just in a kind of certain one, like a sworn vow.'

'And it was.'

'It was. I didn't see how she could do such a thing, but before the week was over she was keeping company with a man named Captain Pruitt.'

'I know who he is,' Walt said. 'The railroad section boss.'

'That's right and apparently they began plotting together. The saloon is the result. I didn't see how this could hurt the Cock's Crow at first,' Rowena said. 'It turned out that Diane had personally ordered and signed for the last shipment of whiskey, in her role as saloon manager. She arranged through Pruitt to have it delivered out here. After a while, the Cock's Crow found it was nearly out of whiskey, had lost its bartenders, some of its girls . . . And a lot more customers than you'd guess. Every worker riding that train now knows where he can get his first drink of the evening, before getting back to Sand Hill. When the line is open to Denver, a lot of men will travel out here just to look the place over along the way. Diane has a lot of friends back in Sand Hill.'

'And it will be the first stop for all of the passengers coming from Denver when that stretch opens.'

'I heard that Diane is going to open a hotel out here.'

'That's always been a part of her plan, yes,' Walt said.

'Men with no place special to go might like staying around in a saloon with cheap whiskey and women to dance with or just look at.'

'There will be gambling, too, no doubt of that. I don't know how Diane will do it, but you can bet she will.'

'She's got a plan, yes. If that's what she said. That's what made her such a good saloon manager. Something Sanders and Pettigrew chose to overlook in their greed.'

Walt stood and dusted himself off. It was time they were getting back to the saloon, even though neither of them had a thing to do there.

'Rowena, you said that you thought that Sanders and Pettigrew had swindled the original owner out of the Cock's Crow.'

'That's what everyone who I talk to says.' They had stopped now by the horses.

'What did you say the man's name was — the original owner?'

'McElroy, David McElroy. I've heard he was the love of Diane's life. It's even said that they were married. I wouldn't know; it was long before I got to Sand Hill.'

'His name was what?' Walt asked.

'David McElroy.' Rowena frowned. 'Why, did you know him?'

'No,' Walt replied, 'but I might have met someone who was related to him.'

He said no more as they started leading the horses back to the saloon. He might have met someone who was a relative. The land was too large for this kind of meeting to be a coincidence, there could only be so many McElroys traipsing the desert.

Clyde's new 'spider' had been introduced as Danny McElroy. The kid had arrived unseen — not from the train, Walt was convinced. Could he have been the mysterious desert rider they had seen, the man who had broken into their storage room for provisions? The man who stayed in the area, having no discoverable reason for being there . . .

Unless it was to find his mother.

The idea seemed far-fetched, but all of the pieces fit together for that being the case. Diane's 'true love', David McElroy, had built up the Cock's Crow in Sand Hill. He had to be by all accounts driven out of business by two men named Art Sanders and Lawrence Pettigrew in what was said to be some kind of swindle.

The same two men drove Diane out of Sand Hill, wanting her percentage of the Cock's Crow's revenue. Diane had set out to show them she would not be so easily handled, and started a saloon of her own in this unlikely, desolate spot.

'Well?' Rowena asked with an edge of nervousness in her voice as they returned the horses to their tethering spot.

'What?' Walt asked, tying the bay to its anchor stone.

'Well, what are we going to do now?'

'You'll have to ask Diane. Probably whatever you used to do at Cock's Crow this time of day.'

'But that man . . . he makes me too nervous, frightened. I don't like being around him.'

'Diane knows that. She'll keep you away from Shannon Pike. If she hasn't any special project for you, just go back to your room and stay there.'

'The door hasn't a lock,' Rowena said, trembling slightly as she looked up at Walt.

'I doubt he'd try to start any tough stuff — this is his last work, too. Who else would hire him? He's known for his nasty disposition. I'll see about getting a lock on your door. The carpenters, at least some of them, are still here this morning.'

'I know, I saw some of them. Did you notice they were all carrying rifles this morning?'

'Rifles? What in the world for?'

'The Colorado & Eastern sent out a notice that someone called Ray John Pettit, a known robber, had been seen in the area.'

'Yes, he has,' Walt said.

Rowena shrugged. 'The railroad doesn't want to take any chances with the man causing trouble for them.'

'Was I Ray John Pettit, I'd be cheering for the railroad to get through to Denver. When they get that line established, it will be bringing refined gold and silver out of that city. Then is the time to hit it, not now.'

'You would have made a good bandit prince,' Rowena said, joking to keep her thoughts away from the perceived menace of Shannon Pike.

'Trouble with that kind of work is that it has no future.'

'You've never been an outlaw, then, Walt?' The question seemed silly, but also seemed to have some importance to Rowena, who had probably not been told the truth often in her life.

'Not until Sand Hill,' he told her. 'A man killed my best friend and I had to pay him back for it.'

'Was that you?' she asked. 'I heard it was a horse that was killed and Vance Hereford was the one who got shot down over it. I knew Vance, he was one of the Cock's Crow dealers . . . he wasn't much of a man, but I knew him. It makes things different somehow.'

'Yes, it does,' Walt said, feeling a little prickly. 'It would have made a difference if you'd known my horse too.'

'Yes, I suppose so,' Rowena said doubtfully.

'That animal was the best friend I had.'

'You must not get around very

much,' Rowena said. She had clouded up a little and Walt was afraid she was going to return to her crying.

'Oh, I've gotten around plenty, the thing is I've never settled anyplace long enough to make a friend, a true friend.'

'I guess I can understand what you mean. I've lived in crowds of strangers — their faces changed, but they might as well have been the same people I'd already met.'

'No true friends?' Walt asked and she knew what he meant by the question.

Rowena looked away and then down, her eyes still misty. She touched Walt's forearm tentatively. Rowena said, 'I guess I'd better talk to Diane and see what she has planned for us.' She turned then to enter the saloon, but her hand gripped Walt's arm very firmly before she went.

Walt pondered for a minute. He was right back in consternation. He knew the territory well, it was where he found himself every time he talked to a woman outside of saying 'howdy'.

Lonely people always seemed to find each other. Walt strode away. There was one young man he wished to talk to. Maybe it was none of his business, but it could be that it was the reason Diane Kingsley had hired Walt to be her bodyguard in the first place.

He wouldn't know until after he had had his talk with young Danny McElroy.

Behind him someone had broken out a harmonica and the tuneless voices of the railroad men followed him up the hill toward the water tower. The saloon was open for business on this day. Rowena would be busy working the job she hated so much.

People always had to settle for so much less than they might have had.

He dismissed Rowena from his mind. She only went with the greatest of efforts.

10

Walt had not exactly burst through the door to Clyde Waring's shack, but he had entered purposefully and Clyde's normally amiable face drew down at the edges.

'Where's that man of yours? Where's Danny McElroy — I want to talk to him.' Walt's voice was stronger than he had intended, but he wanted to talk to Danny and find out once and for all if he was who Walt believed him to be, and if so, why he was going about things the way he was.

'He's out back splitting some of that firewood the railroad delivered, Walt. Why? You look like you've got some serious business on your mind.'

'Pretty serious. But don't worry, Clyde, I didn't come to cause you trouble or bring harm to the boy.'

'Well, that eases my mind some. I just

hope you aren't going to do or say anything to drive the boy off. God and the Colorado and Eastern know when I'll get another spider!'

Walt was already out the door before Clyde had finished his complaint. Was he going to drive Danny away by confronting him? Maybe it was none of his business, but Walt figured Danny as more likely to give him information than Diane Kingsley ever would be, and Walt felt the need to know. He had been living in the blind for too long.

He found Danny where Clyde had indicated he would. With his shirt off, the kid looked terribly thin although he had good muscle tone; he would be a strapping man one day. It couldn't have helped that the kid seemed to have been living off the desert and pilfered scraps for some time now. Why? That was one of the questions he wanted to ask Danny McElroy. There was only one place to begin, and that was with the proper foundation for his other questions.

'Is Diane Kingsley your mother?' Walt asked without preamble and the kid stopped, axe overhead and turned toward Walt, his young face a mask of puzzlement.

'What makes it your business?' the kid asked, gathering his courage. His ax blade descended and split a length of wood cleanly.

'Only one thing,' Walt answered evenly. 'I was hired to protect Diane from any and all threats. I won't let her be harmed.'

The ax rested in silence. Danny McElroy laughed very loudly, briefly. 'You think that I would hurt her?' he asked.

'I just don't know, how would I? Maybe it's you she's hiding from. I don't see anyone else riding on the desert, rifle in hand. And I know you lied to Clyde. He was so eager to get a man, any man, that he believed you even though a railroad man had no business coming out here with a pony, as you did. One you claimed you unloaded on the far side of the train where there aren't even any doors. So, you're secretive and you're a liar.'

Danny bristled at this characterization. Walt continued, 'And most telling of all, a man comes all this way and then spend days skulking about and not going to her, letting her know that he was here.'

'You don't know very much, do you, mister?' Danny said, still sharply but not with terrific anger. 'My mother asked me not to come out here with her; she said there was going to be trouble and she didn't want me involved.'

'Trouble? Surely she couldn't have meant the Ray John Pettit gang. We didn't even know they were around until . . .'

'I knew you didn't know very much. It's not those outlaws — though they gave me a little start. I saw a few of them riding out on the desert while I was trying to decide what to do.'

'Is it something that goes back to

trouble between your mother and your father?' Walt hazarded. 'The reason why you didn't go to her, I mean? She never talks about him.'

Danny McElroy placed his ax aside and sat down on the wood stack, shaking his head as if he could not believe the ignorance of Walt Cassidy.

'Mister, you couldn't be more wrong. My mother loved my father. After those two snakes cheated Dad out of Cock's Crow, he had to go to work — mining was the only work he could find, and both his legs got broke in a cave-in. He was terribly depressed after that. Had to use a wheelchair, said a man who couldn't work and support his family was a useless creature on this earth.

'Mother refused to let it get her down. She was always laughing around the house, and she kept it spotless; she never missed a night's work at the Cock's Crow — ever. She just kept on plodding, taking care of me and Dad, telling him that she would pay back those men who had cheated him one day.'

'Art Sanders and Lawrence Pettigrew.'

'Those are the skunks. Mother told you about them?'

'No. It was someone else. For some reason she never tells me anything. It would help if she did.'

'Help what? Help you go off half-cocked on another crazy idea you plucked out of thin air?'

'You have a point,' Walt was forced to admit. 'I just wanted to know who you were.'

'You have a damned rough way of asking.'

'Yes, I was wrong, and I'm sorry,' Walt said. 'Who, then, was your mother afraid of you getting hurt by if not Ray John Pettit?'

'You have to ask? Mother knows her friends and she knows her enemies. She told me one day Sanders or Pettigrew, one or both of them, would get mad enough at her for the shenanigans she was pulling to wreck the Cock's Crow that she would find them on her doorstep with blood in their eyes. She didn't want me there when it happened.

'Walt, you amaze me. Who did you think you were hired to protect my mother from?'

'I amaze myself sometimes, but Danny, seriously, I never had even heard of these men before the last few days. It's a little clearer now; I just wish I had known all along.' Walt paused. 'I will give you a little advice, after all you've told me. Go along down and say hello to your mother, no matter what you promised not to do. There's no mother in the world who would not be happy to see her wandering son return.'

Danny promised that, but after a fashion. He was still uncertain that Diane would be pleased to see him after she had given him strict orders not to come near the saloon.

Well, on that Danny would have to struggle with his own conscience. Walt had given him the best advice he had, even knowing it had not been asked for, and that he was not the likeliest man to give someone good advice.

Still, Walt felt a little buoyed up now. He at least had an idea of what was going on around him — and exactly what he had been hired to do, and he vowed that he would do whatever it took to protect Diane.

Walt looked in on Clyde on his way by. 'Well,' the old man asked, 'didn't drive him off, did you?'

'No, he's staying. Will you tell me something, Clyde, did you ever really think that the railroad had sent you a spider when Danny showed up?'

'With him arriving on a horse? One he snuck on and off the train? No, Walt — I never thought any such a thing. But I surely was grateful that he showed up.'

At the hotel Diane greeted Walt with 'And where have you been?' the minute he stuck his foot inside the door.

'Oh, I was up talking to your son,' he

said without stopping to expand on the subject. He walked away, thinking Diane would immediately call him back, but she did not.

Jack Green was working the bar, and unsurprisingly there were still two railroad carpenters there, now trying to ease their way out of their hangovers. It seemed they had resigned their jobs or were ready to.

He spoke briefly to the man he knew as Willie to tell him about the job he needed done, then asked Jack Green, 'Where's Toby?'

'Mooning around somewhere. I don't know why the man does this to himself. He was the same way back in Sand Hill.' Walt's head came up sharply at the sound of footsteps descending the staircase.

Here they came in all their glory — the tall, stately looking brunette, wearing a smile as she entered which made her look completely different from the shrew Walt had already met, and Lynn, the smaller girl who, with a splash of rouge, now looked older and more confident.

They went directly to the bar, one at either end and those railroad men who could stood up. An eager Willie was the first man to strike up a conversation with Celia — after ordering her a drink, of course. He might have met her back in Sand Hill at the Cock's Crow, for they entered their conversation easily, not like complete strangers. The railroad carpenter even brought out a laugh from Celia — a pleasing, amused sound. There was no harshness in it, no falsity that Walt could detect. Was it just Walt she hated for no known reason, or was she very good at her job of flattering men?

Lynn was working her game at the opposite end of the bar, now joined by Joe Buck and Arnie. The girl was playing the shy debutante, and doing it very well indeed — after she had been bought a drink, which Walt, watching Jack Green behind the bar, knew was coming from a different bottle than the

men had been swigging down —
saloons were the same everywhere.

Walt started away. Rowena had not
come down which both cheered and
worried him. He gestured to Willie and
got a promising nod. He then went to
the steps and went up them more
quickly than he had intended.

He passed his own room, glanced in
and proceeded next door to Rowena's
where he tapped three times gently.

'Who is it?' a voice with a little
quaver in it enquired.

'It's Walt,' he answered.

'Didn't we just part?' she asked
teasingly. 'Come in.'

She was standing at the window,
looking out at the desert. She turned
slowly. She had not been crying. Her
face was now a mask of determined
desperation. Her features were so
mournful, except for her eyes which
were as hard and unreadable as a
riverboat gambler's. Walt was drawn
uneasily toward her. Uneasily because
he was not sure he wanted to step

inside her unhappiness.

Moving forward, Walt stepped over curling wood chips shaved from the door. They crunched underfoot like beetles.

'Someone named Willie came up here, installed a lock on the door and shaved the edge of it a little.'

'I sent him up. I wasn't sure he'd remember to get to it.'

'Thank you,' Rowena answered in a voice so flat that Walt wondered for a moment if the girl had been drinking some of the saloon's whiskey. But it was nothing like that; she seemed to just have lost some of her natural vigor, her spirit as had the gray horse that had arrived, ridden into the ground.

Walt looked at the littered floor. 'In my experience, carpenters dislike cleaning up after themselves almost as much as a cowboy does being asked to do any out-of-the saddle job.'

'He was in a hurry. I told him I'd sweep up later.'

'Oh,' Walt replied, always a clever man in conversation. He was standing close to Rowena now, the heated wind fluttering through the window. There was still no glass in the windows and a small disoriented hawk flew in past the curtains and circled the room. Walt got the bird back on track with a wave of his hat.

Rowena twisted around as if she were having a small fit and settled on the bed, looking up at Walt in apology. 'I didn't mean to cower like a schoolmarm.' Walt, who had known a few very tough schoolmarms, didn't answer. What Rowena resembled more was a fearful girl on her first day at work in a saloon.

Her look became a challenge. 'I'm not going to cry, so you can quit waiting for that.'

'No — Rowena, I had no idea you were so close to the end of the line, or I wouldn't have made light of it.'

'It's nothing you did or didn't do, Walt. I had a good look at myself sitting in a store room crying my eyes out — for what? Now I've made a decision. If working in saloons is making me so miserable, I'm just going to quit. That's it. No more!'

'I wondered why you didn't come down with the other girls.'

Rowena went on as if she had not heard him.

'Tomorrow — or is it the next day? — I am going to grab a small suitcase and ride the train to Denver. I don't know what I shall do there. Maybe I'll marry a copper king — or some dimwitted stablehand. It really wouldn't matter which. Just so I had a place to be.'

'You have a place now,' Walt reminded her.

'No, I don't. You should understand better than anyone, Walt — this is no place.'

'Just the end of the line,' Walt said.

'Just a dumping-off place. I don't know how to tell Diane that I made a mistake agreeing to come out here with the others. Maybe you could tell her for me, Walt.'

'No, you had better talk to her face to face.' Walt took her hand and patted it, looking into the girl's eyes, just to give her that last little bit of confidence she needed. 'Maybe you could hire me for the job I'm doing now for Diane,' Walt suggested. 'I'm ready to leave myself, as you know; maybe we could both take the train to Denver tomorrow.'

'Maybe we . . . what do you mean hire you? I can't afford to pay anything to anyone!'

'That's the same pay I'm getting now.'

Rowena's face screwed up in puzzlement. 'Well, what are you doing now? Why would I need you?'

'I was joking about that part, Rowena, but not about riding with you to Denver. I'm ready; I'm past ready. My job now is a sort of bodyguard to Diane Kingsley. I figure I could do that for you until you found yourself a copper king . . . or a stablehand.'

'Now you're still kidding, right?'

'Only if you are. I'd be happy to sort of take care of you for a while — they tell me Denver can be a rough town.'

'Are you doing this for me, or for yourself?' Rowena asked with suspicion.

'I always keep my mind only on the job — my last employer will give me a reference.'

He stood, smiling, and after a while she returned it, standing to join him.

'I hardly know how to answer,' Rowena said.

'You don't have to,' Walt replied. 'You can decide along the way or in Denver . . . or never. It doesn't matter. But I'm riding through to Denver if they'll sell me a ticket.'

'Why wouldn't they? No one could hold a grudge that long.'

'You've never met Tug Travis,' Walt said. 'They've likely telegraphed all the stations along the route not to allow me aboard.'

'You're teasing again, aren't you? I have trouble keeping up with your sense of humor. Besides, you've a good friend running things here.'

'Yeah, I guess Clyde would allow me to sneak aboard a freight car.'

'A freight car?' Rowena was still wearing that face that meant she couldn't tell if Walt was kidding or not. 'Why can't you just buy a ticket?'

'Seems simple, doesn't it? The answer is I haven't got two nickels to rub together. Which is a matter I have to clear up right now. Let's go, Rowena,' he said, extending a hand. 'There's a few things we both need to talk about to Diane Kingsley before the morning train leaves.'

11

The morning was still gray when Walt Cassidy tapped at Rowena's door and was admitted to find the girl already dressed in a plain brown outfit suited to the event. The lantern on the table was lighted, burning very low. Her suitcases were on the bed, packed.

'I see you haven't changed your mind overnight,' he said.

'No, though I shared some anxious moments with myself. You haven't changed your mind, either?'

'Not me,' Walt said lightly. 'I haven't got that much of a mind to make up, so it doesn't take much to go with what I have planned and just march ahead.'

'I just kept thinking I was going from *somewhere* to nowhere,' Rowena said. Nearer now, Walt could see the signs of sleeplessness on her — she had sat up all night long, worrying.

'You might have that backward, Rowena. There is a lot of somewhere ahead in Denver, and there's nothing at all here, never will be.'

'I know,' she said with a faint, uneasy smile, 'the end of the line.'

'The beginning,' Walt corrected. 'Come on, let's get started,' he said, taking her hand.

'Diane won't be in her room.'

'I know that,' Walt said. He had been around the woman long enough to know that Diane Kingsley looked on time spent sleeping as time being wasted. If she was not actually asleep, she was busy with her planning which seemed endless.

'Maybe we should have brought that lantern with us,' Walt said as they made their way down to the saloon, feeling their way along by using the banister. There was some bright lamp burning somewhere below, but there was no telling where. The store room, Walt thought.

They had just stepped down to the

saloon floor when the front door was swung open with violence and the tumult began.

'I'll have it back, Diane, every bit of it!' a man yelled from the front of the saloon.

'I don't know what you mean,' Diane Kingsley's measured voice responded.

They hurried that way, Walt being painfully aware that he had not strapped on his gun belt this morning, feeling no need for it when their object was meeting with Diane in an empty saloon. Now and then Walt had to remind himself that there was no telling what a new morning might bring.

On this morning it had brought a furious stranger who stood framed in the doorway against the dull light of the desert pre-dawn. He had a booming voice, and was a large man, not a fat one. He had pomaded hair which must have been neatly brushed at some time before his long ride across the desert.

'Here, what's this?' Walt bellowed,

aware of both duty and his missing Colt.

He gave Rowena a gentle shove out of the way. He did not know what this intruder's problem was, but he was obviously the sort to let his anger run away with him — and he was angry. And armed. A revolver dangled from his fist.

As Rowena stumbled aside, he heard her whisper throatily, 'Art Sanders.'

So that's who the big man was: one of the owners of the Cock's Crow Saloon in Sand Hill.

'Where's the charming Mr Pettigrew?' Diane asked the saloon owner, glancing in Walt's direction.

'In his bed, no doubt. You know my partner — he hasn't got the stomach for anything like this.'

'Like what?' she asked. 'What exactly is it you're up to, Art?'

'Repossession. Diane, my dear,' Sanders said, taking a menacing step nearer to Diane, 'you and your cohorts have stolen half of the Cock's Crow, piece by piece.' He noticed Rowena for the first time, 'Aha, there's another bit of your booty. Where are the other stolen girls? I need them to bring in customers, as you well know. And where's little Toby? He has to be around here somewhere. What about Jack Green? Is he here, too? This is my bar, isn't it, with my whiskey casks behind it?'

'I can't remember where I came by that,' Diane said easily as if the big man with the gun in his hand was only a trivial annoyance.

'I was wondering why you were playing up to that Captain Pruitt of the railroad; now I guess I know. Planning ahead for the time you might need him. You are an unscrupulous woman, Diane Kingsley.'

'I was just taking what was mine. Why don't you just chalk it up to experience and leave before I have to turn my bodyguard loose on you, Art?'

Of course in that light Diane could not know that Walt was unarmed. If he had been, what was he to do, just shoot the obnoxious saloon owner down? Rowena touched his arm lightly and he glanced down to see the terror in her eyes.

'Turn him loose,' Art Sanders said carelessly. 'I've got to make my stand somewhere; it might as well be here.'

'You've made your choice,' a not unfamiliar voice roared. 'And if that's the way you want it, you can have it. No sense bringing out the big guns, Miss Kingsley.'

Shannon Pike appeared in the store room door, oddly lighted by the sky which was gathering milky color. Sanders took a step back. Pike was a known quantity to him. He had fired Pike from the Cock's Crow for his unrestrained violence.

'I'm giving you a choice, Sanders,' Pike said advancing. 'If you want a fight, you can have it with fists, guns or knives. I'm betting I can beat you with all three.'

The bouncer's voice was tight, his

eyes narrowed. Walt knew, Sanders knew, that Pike was not kidding. Violence was what he did to earn a living, did because he liked it.

'You have a bowie on your belt, Sanders? If not and you want to go to steel, I'll have someone bring you a spare one of mine.' He paused, breathing roughly as if making a difficult decision. He glanced at Diane Kingsley who had backed up a little, but had no hint of uneasiness about her.

'Well, we've already got a good little graveyard out back. How many men buried there, Walt? Three?'

'Four, ma'am.'

'Plenty of room,' she said as if talking to herself, though her remarks were obviously meant for Art Sanders's ears.

'I don't feel like digging,' Pike said like a sullen child. 'Let's just finish this here and now. 'Your choice, Sanders. You can either leave by the front door or the back. I'm through playing. You may not have a knife, but you've got

194

two feet, use them now or I will assist you. Go! Miss Kingsley don't want her floor all bloody.'

Pike took one more step forward and the sand ran out of Art Sanders — he had once employed Pike and knew too much of him. With one muffled curse, Art Sanders turned and started toward the front door, glancing back across his shoulder. After a few hesitant minutes, they heard Sanders's horse being ridden away.

Shannon Pike, still dressed in jeans and a long john shirt, strutted as he walked to where the cold-eyed Diane Kingsley stood, watching after Art Sanders's receding horse. A spark of crimson flashed against the dull sky. They were ready to meet the dawn.

Walt had not heard Rowena approach again, but now she clung to his arm. 'I am so glad you weren't wearing your gun this morning. It would have been an awful way to begin our new day.'

Diane Kingsley remembered now

that the two had come down from upstairs to see her, and she turned to study them for a moment.

'Need something?' she asked.

'Yes, Miss Kingsley. We've both come to check out,' Walt told her. 'The train today is making its first run to Denver — you always knew I was pulling up stakes as soon as I could get along down the road.'

'Yes, I knew that, Walt. That's why I couldn't bring myself to let you go. I knew a morning like this was coming, that someone from Sand Hill would come looking for me, and I wanted you around for protection.'

'Fat lot of protecting he was good for,' Shannon Pike said. He was still preening. 'When it came down to shove or shy, you saw who you could count on.' He gave Walt a dark look which said, 'I guess I showed you who the big dog is around here.'

Walt ignored him.

So did Diane Kingsley. It just wasn't that important to either of them what

Shannon Pike thought. People who talk loud, cuss and scream never seem to realize that it doesn't impress anyone or mean that you've won an argument. Folks just seem to block all that out of their thoughts.

'Finish getting yourself dressed, Pike,' Diane said. 'Then maybe you could spend a few minutes outside making sure that Art Sanders isn't crazy enough to come back here again.'

Pike nodded silently, shot a dark, prideful look at Walt Cassidy and stamped off toward the store room where he had been sleeping on one of the spare mattresses. After a few minutes things were back to normal. Toby had reappeared, and the carpenters who had been sleeping in the back wandered toward the bar, apparently awakened by Pike's clumping around back there. Toby had poured these shaky men each a drink before they had even asked, brightening their outlook on the new day.

Walt remembered to say, 'Thanks for the lock, Willie.'

''S nothin'. Hope the lady sleeps better now.'

'All right, refugees,' Diane said with a meager smile for Walt and Rowena, 'Let's get our business taken care of. Wait until Pike leaves then come into the store room to join me.'

'In the store room?' Walt asked, confused.

'That's where my safe is. If you want to get paid, follow me.' Rowena and Walt glanced at each other, looked toward the front door where Pike had exited, buttoning his shirt, and trailed Diane dutifully to the storage room which was now deserted. The room was still dark enough in the far corners that a lantern would have been welcome. Diane threw open the rear door, letting meager dawn light beam in.

Diane went immediately to a front corner of the room where a single ham hung from the rafters and a coil of pork sausage was dangling from a nail in the wall.

'Over here, Walt. I want you to pry up this plank. Grab one of those shovels.'

Walt did as he was told and went to where Diane waited somewhat impatiently.

'Which . . . ?' was as far as he got with his question. Diane was toeing a narrow plank with an 'X' crudely, shallowly scratched on it.

'That one,' she said.

Walt nodded and slipped the blade of the shovel between the plank and its neighbor and pried. It took very little effort to raise the plank. Diane got to her knees, glanced toward the door and swiftly removed a pair of saddle bags which lay concealed there. Walt thought he recognized the ones the mysterious dying rider had been carrying when he arrived at the saloon aboard the crippled gray horse.

'Put it back, dust a little material over it — I may need to use the cache again sometime. Neat little place, is it not?

The carpenters made it for me.'

'But — ' Walt began.

'Save it, Walt. I never answer your questions anyway, do I? Let's get up to your room and see to this.'

He shrugged, felt Rowena take his arm again, and they followed Diane up the stairs. Diane Kingsley told him, 'If you're worried about the train, don't be. It won't pull in for another half an hour.' Then she turned, closed the door carefully and seated herself on the bed.

'As you know, Walt, a friend of mine delivered these to me. Why don't you belt on your pistol and gather whatever belongings you have?'

'I'll have to get Rowena's suitcases.'

'They'll wait a few minutes,' Diane said, studying them both steadily for a long minute before her left eye began to wander. She slapped at her forehead with annoyance at her body's refusal to obey her commands. 'You two are saying goodbye, I assume. Well, I expected it. Walt, he was ready to go before I even got here! Rowena — I somehow thought things would be easier out here for you than they were in Sand Hill. At least you'd have your friends around you still. I didn't realize how much you hated the whole business, not just Cock's Crow. It was a mistake to ask you to come along with Celia and Lynn.

'Or maybe it did all work out for the best. You've stopped crying at least. I had an older woman tell me once that if you didn't cry for a man, you didn't love him; I think it's a lot better to meet one who can keep you from crying.'

She glanced at Walt who did not respond and at Rowena, who was a little flushed now.

'Well, that's none of my business but only your own,' Diane said, going to the window, perhaps looking down the long tracks for the train, or further, into her past life. Abruptly she said, 'Get your suitcases, Rowena, and make sure you haven't left anything behind. Look around carefully — you know how some small item that matters is lost when you move.'

'I'll do it,' Walt said, turning toward the door.

'No. I think Rowena had better do it. You and I have some business to discuss, Walt.'

He cocked his head to look at her, then nodded. Rowena slipped from the room, slightly confused. 'All right, then, Diane. What is it?'

'Let me look in these first,' she said, reaching for the saddle bags. She patted the bed for Walt to sit down opposite her. 'You know who brought these, but you don't know why — I don't think I'll tell you.'

'No matter,' Walt answered. Her statement was no surprise to him. He was just growing anxious about leaving . . . how he was going to leave? Diane flashed one of her brighter smiles.

'I owe you for weeks of work here, Walt.'

'I can't say I've really done much,' he said.

'You eased my mind in ways you

couldn't know,' Diane said.

'That's just because I didn't say everything I was thinking.'

'You said enough. I know it was torture to you to remain here. The saloon was always my dream, mine and no one else's. I do know how much you wanted a horse, a way to get away from here and try starting a new life as you want it. Well, you've got more reason now, Walt,' she said, glancing at the party open door. 'Promise me you won't hurt the girl.'

'Hurt her! That's the last thing I have in mind, Diane.'

'And the first thing?' Diane asked, avoiding his eyes.

'Just to get her safely to Denver, try to find her a decent place to live. After that . . . We haven't discussed after that. It's too soon to know such things.'

Diane studied Walt intently for a long half a minute. 'All right, Walt, take this,' she said, handing the heavy saddle bags to him. 'It'll give both of you a little cushion to start on. You'll at least have a hotel bed and meals. You'll get your horse finally. Make it a good one. I did feel bad about that, Walt, honestly.'

'All right,' Walt answered with some doubt. 'As you say, all I ever wanted was a horse to get along down the trail. Rowena — she might need a little help for a while, more than I can give her.' He looked deliberately at Diane. 'She was talking about marrying the first man who asked her. I guess she was pretty tired of herself.'

'And the saloon,' Diane said. She stood up. 'Take those saddle bags and tuck them away. No need to look in them now. That old Number Eight should be arriving soon. Good luck in Denver . . . I hope it's the better life you're both hoping for.'

Distantly the train whistle blew, resounding across the desert, announcing its arrival to the men manning the water tank. Rowena stood nervously in the hallway. The time had arrived, and as with any long-expected event, the actual moment's arrival left her nearly confused.

It was at that moment that they heard a rifle shot from beyond the walls of the saloon. Toby Riggs, panting, his face fearful and white, arrived at the top of the stairs.

'They're coming,' he panted, 'Pike is going to need some help.'

'Who's coming?' Diane asked with practiced coolness.

'Why, Diane, dear,' Toby blurted out without thinking, 'it's the Ray John Pettit gang, looking for whiskey, money and women.'

'What can we do?' Diane Kingsley asked, her face now showing strain.

'We'll have to find that out,' Toby answered. 'We're going to war, that's for sure, and if we let Ray John win, he'll destroy everything you've worked so hard to build up. He'll take your liquor and your women and burn the saloon to the ground.'

12

For once Diane seemed lost and indecisive. Everyone was looking to her for leadership, but this was beyond her. Half a dozen shots, nearer, racketed across the desert. From below, a scattering of shots sang out inside the saloon. Rowena's eyes studied Walt urgently, seeking aid. Her dream was suddenly turning to ashes.

'Let's get to it, Toby,' Walt said. He had already started down the stairs. The shots from within became louder as they descended. Walt caught sight of an extremely nervous Jack Green firing his rifle out the front window. Shannon Pike knelt before another window, and he glanced at Walt with a sort of murderous glee on his face. Pike was in his glory; the killing time was here.

'Check the back door,' Pike said, assuming command. 'There's no one back there but Willie. I think they got the other one, Joe Buck. It seems old Joe quit the railroad a day too early.'

Nearing Pike in a crouch, Walt wanted to know, 'How many are there?'

'Plenty of them. Twenty, thirty, maybe. It seems like Ray John is bringing all he's got this time.'

'I'll get to the store room,' Walt said, rushing that way, keeping his head low. He and Pike detested each other, but each of them knew that they had an ally they could count on in a fight.

Toby followed Walt, and they reached the store room just in time to see the carpenter, Willie, take a shot in the shoulder and whirl around, cursing as the blood started flowing from a wound in his shoulder.

'Get down!' Walt shouted as Toby dove to the floor behind several stacks of dried beans and corn meal. Willie reacted too slowly and he was tagged by another bullet which struck him at the belt just above his right hip. He slumped to the floor beneath the window as Walt took over his position, approaching the window carefully.

Lifting his eyes above the sill, Walt could see that three Pettit riders had taken their positions behind the sand dunes. It was not prime shelter, and they showed no inclination to move or attempt rushing the hotel. Still they kept up a steady, measured volley.

Walt fired one almost meaningless shot meant only to keep their heads down. From the front of the saloon, he could hear the steady reports of Shannon Pike's Winchester. That side was protected, at least for now. The raucous whistle of Number Eight blatted again, much nearer now. The volume of the arriving train was rising almost as much as the rifle fire from the war outside.

'He means business,' Toby panted, meaning Ray John Pettit.

'Yes, he does. I was wondering if he wanted the train,' Walt said as he ducked following the whine of a ricochet near at hand.

'How could he know when the train gets here?'

'He's had men out there scouting around for days,' Walt agreed, but something about it did not seem right.

'Anyway, it's the saloon they're coming after. Let's give them cause to resent it.'

The wounded Willie said from the floor beside them, 'Give 'em hell, boys!'

Walt and Toby began to do just that, peppering the white sand desert with round after round of .44-40s. The outlaws they had cornered there rose up only occasionally to fire back. Doubtless the men were already sorry they had taken up their position there, lying on the hot sand with scant cover. And the sand and sun could only get hotter. Soon it would be an oven out there. Hearing a small rustling sound, Walt glanced behind him to see Rowena crouched over Willie.

'What are you doing here?' Walt asked angrily, wiping the perspiration from his eyes.

'Trying to help. I'm better at nursing than shooting.'

'Then get down!' he shouted as a few more shots spun jagged lead through the room, one bullet catching the smoked ham on the butt.

'Are they all right out front? Who's holding the fort?' Willie asked.

'Pike — I think he's enjoying himself, Jack Green who's showing a lot more nerve than I would have given the little man credit for. And Diane,' Rowena said, 'I'll give her her due. She grabbed a rifle and got to work — I saw her drop one man. She knows what she's doing with that weapon.'

'I'd guess so. Diane Kingsley has probably traveled a lot of rough trails we'll never know about,' Walt said.

The firing from the front of the saloon seemed to be tapering off. One of the men they had pinned behind the sand dun now got to his feet and made a mad dash for escape. Toby Riggs dropped him with a snap shot and the outlaw tumbled to the sand.

Simultaneously there was a fierce barrage of rifle fire from the front of the house, and leaving Toby to watch the back windows, Walt scurried for the front through the saloon hall which was thick with black powder smoke now.

In a crouch, he moved to the front window beside Diane who glanced at him but said nothing.

Walt said, 'They tagged Willie, but it looks like he'll make it. What's happening out there?' He was yelling to make himself heard above the wave of gunfire, but it became more unnecessary as the shooting died down, only a sporadic shot sounding now and then.

'A trainload full of railroad men with rifles is what happened,' Diane said. 'Help me up, Walt, will you? My knees creak a little these days. Even Ray John Pettit isn't crazy enough to charge thirty men. There's a lot of dead bodies out there and I do owe those railroaders a few drinks.'

'That'll teach those bastards,' Pike

said, standing to stretch. A last shot, like the echo of a dead battle, sounded and Pike nodded amiably and fell over dead.

Diane said, 'The lunatic got what he has been chasing for so long.' She looked at Pike, not with sorrow for the man, but for all the men living their meaningless lives on a trail leading to a meaningless death.

'You can't stop them and you can't slow them down,' Diane said with deep regret.

There was a rumpus outside the front door and a shoulder was thrown against it. The man who limped in was dressed all in black. He dragged his leg slightly. His face was tanned to the color of leather, cut with the lines of desert living. He had a Colt revolver in his hand.

'You know me too well, Diane. You can't think I'd run away. Now, where is it?'

'I don't know, Ray John,' Diane Kingsley said calmly.

212

'I'll find it.'

'I doubt it. You'd do better riding. There's probably thirty men out there. You've been running your luck too thin for a long time.'

'I've got more . . . you, cowboy, hit the flip and whirl that pistol aside!'

That was exactly what Walt did. Ray John Pettit had the drop on him and he wasn't kidding. Ray John glanced at Walt, but his gaze was kept fixed on Diane.

He stepped forward and grabbed Diane roughly by the throat. 'Now. We're through playing.'

And the game was at an end, for Ray John Pettit. His last threat was uttered around a mouthful of blood. A thundering shot echoed through the empty saloon and Ray John's knees gave out under him. From the other side of the saloon floor, a shadowy figure moved slowly toward them.

His gun was now lowered, barrel trickling smoke. Danny McElroy stumped his way toward them. He was not injured, but the amount of gun smoke and sand on his young body showed that he had been a participant in the gunfight outside. The blond kid walked directly to his mother. Walt heard him mutter, 'I told you years ago to never touch my mother, Ray John.' Then he proceeded to Diane's welcoming arms. There were tears in her eyes as she hugged her missing boy.

To Walt and Rowena she shouted, 'Oh go on and get, you two. They won't hold that train forever!'

The train seemed like some comforting illusion. Were they really on board, ready to plunge into a new life? They did not allow themselves to think about what that might mean — a life away from the bonds of saloon life.

'I don't know what Ray John was thinking, charging a trainload of armed men,' Walt said. Here and there beyond the windows a few trainmen were still trying to clean up the last remnants of the firestorm — the dead.

'He never wanted the train, only the saloon,' Rowena believed.

In another few minutes the brass bell which perched on Number Eight's boiler chirped four times. It was time they were going. Rowena leaned back and snuggled nearer to Walt's arm. Rowena had been thinking about Walt's last comment all this time.

'It doesn't matter, does it, Walt? About Ray John — whether he was hell-bent on reaching the saloon, burning it to the ground, whether he just wanted something he thought Diane had taken from him — his money, or even his son! Who knows?'

Walt didn't know why but the same thought about Danny McElroy had occurred to him. He did not answer Rowena; both were content to leave the past ghosts to the past, entombed in the saloon.

He had taken the time, just as Number Eight began its great iron rush forward, to open the saddle bags Diane had given to him.

'Will we be OK in Denver for a while?' Rowena asked.

Walt had been sifting the gold coins he now seemed to own through his fingers.

'Quite a while,' he told Rowena. 'Don't be in any hurry to throw yourself into a stableman's arms.'

The train was up to speed and it raced on across the long desert toward Denver City, leaving any sight of the saloon behind on the naked desert.

We do hope that you have enjoyed reading this large print book.

Did you know that all of our titles are available for purchase?

We publish a wide range of high quality large print books including:
Romances, Mysteries, Classics
General Fiction
Non Fiction and Westerns

Special interest titles available in large print are:
The Little Oxford Dictionary
Music Book, Song Book
Hymn Book, Service Book

Also available from us courtesy of Oxford University Press:
Young Readers' Dictionary
(large print edition)
Young Readers' Thesaurus
(large print edition)

For further information or a free brochure, please contact us at:
Ulverscroft Large Print Books Ltd.,
The Green, Bradgate Road, Anstey,
Leicester, LE7 7FU, England.
Tel: (00 44) **0116 236 4325**
Fax: (00 44) **0116 234 0205**

Other titles in the
Linford Western Library:

BITTER IS THE DUST

Scott A. Gese

When Sarah McKinney finally escapes the clutches of her abusive husband, she and her adopted son Jason begin a perilous new life on the run. Eventually they settle down as Sarah finds work as a doctor's assistant, and Jason is reunited with his real father and takes a job as a ranch hand. But Jason's quick temper soon gets him into trouble with his employer, and their future hangs in the balance as their unhappy past threatens to catch up with them.